Fuss !

Fuss !

Dr. Chandler has also written:

55 Glimpses: Mark's Record of the Life and Ministry of Jesus

AND,

Certainly Not!

And,

A Men's Journal

Fuss !

Fuss !

Fuss !

REVISED January 2022

> *"The challenge of <u>dying to self</u> and <u>knowing when to stand</u>."*
>
> # Dr. Ben Chandler

Fuss! Fuss! Fuss!

Fuss! Fuss! Fuss!

Fuss, Fuss, Fuss

Copyright © 2022
Ben Chandler

All Scripture quotations unless otherwise indicated are taken from *The New King James Bible Version* ®. Copyright © 1979, 1980, 1982, Thomas Nelson, Inc.

Library of Congress Number:

ISBN: 9798796606216

Imprint: Independently published

Also available in eBook for:
Amazon Kindle, $9.99

Cover Design: Ben Chandler
Interior Design: Ben Chandler

Additional copies of this book are available by mail. Quantity in special price – ask author!

Spiritual Measure Ministries
79 Plantation Lane
Ashville, AL 35953

Printed in the United States of America

Fuss!   Fuss!   Fuss!

Contents

Introduction   **1**

Chapter One   **11**
The Futility of the Fuss

Chapter Two   **37**
Dying to a Futile Experience

Chapter Three   **47**
The Friction of a Fuss

Chapter Four   **61**
Standing in the midst of Friction

Chapter Five   **75**
The Family Fussing

Chapter Six   **87**
Dying for and Standing for Family

Chapter Seven   **99**
The Faithful Fussing

Chapter Eight   **133**
Dying to Self to be Faithful
 and Standing with the Faithful

Chapter Nine   **147**
The Future Fuss

Chapter Ten   **169**
Standing for the Future

Chapter Eleven   **191**
The Flight from Fussing

Chapter Twelve   **209**
Standing as you Flee

Chapter Thirteen   **225**
Forgiveness for the Fuss

Chapter Fourteen   **235**
Dying to Self in order to Forgive

Conclusion   **245**

Addendum   **249**

Appendix   **251**

Fuss! Fuss! Fuss!

ACKNOWLEDGEMENTS

I want to thank my dear, precious wife, Patricia, for the encouragement she has provided me to write these many years. She is beautiful and the love of my life. I have found great blessing in the years of marriage and friendship. With her I find inspiration and the joy of living a life committed to our Lord and Savior Jesus Christ. She is my confidant, my counsellor and true love.

I am blessed to have two of the best human beings on the planet as my children – Dana and David. They are committed to their family and church. I appreciate my children for the many times we have had to draw upon each other's love and forgiveness when faced with those conflicts in life which could destroy relationships. Our children were full of grace and found the strength to talk things out with me and with each other in order to maintain our family togetherness. And, now of course life is richer because of the grandchildren we enjoy. The times we spend with Hannah, Abby, Cole, Lucy and Emma are refreshing and they remind us of so many wonderful things we experienced with our children. They also help us explore new dimensions of life that we never conceived before they arrived. I do appreciate wonderful, precious grandchildren for the many lessons they have taught me about this subject. They have helped me see life for real. They also have shown me how easy it is to forgive and move on with life. I am thankful for a Godly son-in-law, Paul, who knows how to be a peacemaker and guide his children to do the same. I am blessed to have the Triplets mom, Kimberly, as my daughter-in-law, always ready for a challenge and faces life facing forward.

I appreciate the many church leaders who have helped me understand that life is constantly changing and is very short. Some did not know they were teaching me about relationships which have eternal consequences.

Fuss! Fuss! Fuss!

Fuss!   Fuss!   Fuss!

Introduction

Fuss. . .

Fuss. . .

Fuss!!!

"That's all I ever hear!"

Imagine that! My daddy said those words many times. His voice still rings in my ears. I was guilty as we did fuss a lot as kids.   He did hear it multiplied by his five children. But that was not all he ever heard. It just seemed that way to him at times. However, the fussing we experienced as siblings shaped the way we now handle conflict as adults. It does in everyone.

1

My Daddy's statement is one of frustration and anguish. Somehow my Daddy, as good and loving a father as he was, did not have the expertise to "stop" our fussing. He tried. He did it temporarily, until the next big difference came up between me and one of my four siblings or between two of them. Just when a fuss was heated to the max, and Daddy heard it, we could be sure to hear him say, "Fuss, Fuss, Fuss! That is all I ever hear!"

This book is NOT just a book about family feuding, **BUT RATHER** the conflict and fighting that is going on throughout our nation and across the earth.

Our world is a cosmopolitan FUSS!

The fussing heard around the globe has inspired the spiritual response found in this book. Fussing on a national scale has many of the same dynamics as fussing by two individuals.

Fuss! Fuss! Fuss!

People will continue to fuss until Jesus Christ returns to earth and rules as King of Kings and Lord of Lords.

This book does not have the intent to "stop" the world from fussing. I can't and neither can any human, no matter how powerful.

But rather what you read here is intended by the author to give anyone in the world insights and tools on how NOT to fuss and how to be free of the guilt resulting from a fussing lifestyle. It is designed to help business leaders end conflict among their employees. It also offers the reader insight on how this world will be consummated by a huge fuss.

I married a very level headed woman and she has always been one to know how to diffuse a situation to prevent a fuss. She is always the one to urge me to calm down, be patient and listen. In light of my Daddy's frustration, and because as a Christian Dad, I wanted my home to be free of the "Fuss," we took some solid steps in solving that futile predicament. Oh, we had some arguments! But, none of our arguments were "barn burners" or the kind where our relationships were in jeopardy. The fussing my kids engaged in, did not result in lasting bitterness, or fuming spirits against each other. Fussing took place for sure. But, there was a conclusion to them.

You may be a business man with two or two thousand employees who from time to time disagree and find themselves in a brawl. This book can help you be a peacemaker and preserve your business associates.

As parents we had to make a plan for dealing with fussing. Some of the training I received in college while earning a degree in Elementary Education helped with the solution. I knew as a parent; and I believe all parents today need to come to the same conclusion (Yes, I believe in absolutes), that I could not afford to turn my head when fussing happened between my kids. Hoping it would "work itself out," or that "one of the kids would give in and be okay" were not options for me. I had to have a plan.

We simply applied the principles of trust and sharing we used in our successful experience with fussing.

So, when the kids got into a fuss, I insisted that,

4

1. They had to come up with a solution between themselves and present that to me for approval. I taught them to do some critical thinking, some self-evaluation, and some diplomacy in getting along. We would talk it over and the two of them would agree on what to say and do.

Or,

2. They had to yield to my solution which was usually negotiable and agreeable to everyone's satisfaction.

Fathers make a terrible mistake when they mandate stuff to their kids just to get a quick fix to the fuss. So do managers, and foremen, and key leaders. At the other end of the spectrum is the father or leader who simply lets the offspring argue and feud showing no parental/business authority whatsoever. As someone noted years ago, "If our children do not learn to obey earthly parents whom they can see, how will they ever learn to obey the Heavenly Father whom they cannot see?" Discipline and submission are keys to success in life.

Allow me to share one of the best techniques we used as parents to prevent fussing between our kids. It was when they were old enough to decide they wanted to "ride shotgun" – you know, sit in the front seat by the window (when cars had bench seats, even). Someone would claim "I called it first!" Or, one would cry, "You always get to sit there!" to which the other would say, "Well, I got here first." Then, whoever had to "ride in the back" sulked for a while, and pretty much spoiled an otherwise perfect day.

Solution came when I declared: "Okay, starting Sunday (being the first day of the week) the oldest will get to ride 'shotgun' all week when the two of you ride together, whether I drive or Mom drives. The next week, starting Sunday, Son you get your turn at 'shotgun.' " This continued until the oldest got a driver's permit. There was no more problem all those years. They were honest kids, kept up with whose week it was and we had no more fussing about it.

So, our family found success in other matters, when anything that required sharing came up. We simply applied the principles of trust and sharing that we found successful during times of fussing. When our kids saw that we could be fair, honest and loving, they together solved the problem and there was joy in the camp. Today, their kids enjoy the same experience of sharing.

The Bible declares, "Joy comes in the morning" (Psalm 30:5). For many people, however, when they awake, it is not joy and peace, but an ugly remembrance of the fuss or the fight they engaged in the night or day before. They then set out from the brink of the new day to forward their fuss. They plan ways to "win" the fuss by scheming, plotting and employing immature, unwise and sometimes unGodly behavior. They live with sickness and pain as a result of the

> For many, when they awake, it is not joy and peace. . .

sinfulness of a fuss. Schemes and devices of evil are laid out to entrap the other person. Sometimes it is an innocent spouse or child who becomes the victim of the fussing. In the larger context of the verse mentioned above, (Psalm 30:5) we see God's model for us in responding to anger – many times the root cause of a fuss. "For His anger *is but for* a moment, His favor *is for* life; Weeping may endure for a night, But joy *comes* in the morning." Psalm **30:5 (NKJV)**

The cure is to deny self and bring glory to God. It is my desire to help you the reader and all those you care about find that joy and peace which comes when we learn to die to self and stand for Christ.

Who dies? The person desires to be Christ-like will seek to die to selfishness and any sinful pride that is promoting the fuss. Who stands? Though it may not appear to be so, the one who becomes the peacemaker, stands. The one who strives to resolve the fussing is the victor.

Fussing highlights the spiritual depth and conviction of the individual. The Bible is replete with guidelines for dealing with the issue of fussing. The world is in great conflict. The fussing of a global community will mark the end of time on earth. ONE day the world will experience a huge fuss apart from the church as God removes His people from that fuss.

In this book, a revised edition – since so much of the world has changed and since "fussing" seems to be the norm in all societies; **I hope to show the reader some truths about fussing.** The truths emerge from Biblical study, personal experiences and wisdom gleaned from other sources. It is my desire for every reader to see the influence and sometimes ugly scarring that comes from fussing. In addition, we will consider how to be reconciled with someone we "fussed" with. Then we will look at this "dead end street futility" by learning some things about spiritual warfare, and the cultural battles we must fight. I want you the reader to learn how fussing is simply futile; that there can be an end to the fighting between people; see some of the examples of the family of faith fussing and how that is detrimental to our witness; and last of all how to find and give forgiveness for the wrong and hurt usually found in a fuss. If you want to grow through the conflict that surrounds you in your Christian walk, become a more of a peacemaker and not just a peacekeeper at work, at play, or at home, hang tough and we will get to the truth that sets us free.

The challenge of dying to self and knowing when to stand.

Fuss!   Fuss!   Fuss!

Chapter 1

The Futility of a Fuss

"FUSSING!" What good does it do?

Why bother?

Is there value in feuding?

Who wins? What about the loser?

Losing an argument or quarrel can be serious. The futility of a fuss is sometimes seen in the countenance of the losing party after the fuss. You have witnessed it, I'm sure. The losing person becomes sad, shoulders droop, mouth turns downward, the head bends forward a bit, the eyes sometimes water or the pupils gets smaller. Futility is sometimes seen in the arrogance and superior demeanor of the one who wins the quarrel.

11

Where does it come from? James, the apostle says,

> **Where do wars and fights *come* from among
> you? Do *they* not *come* from your *desires for*
> pleasure that war in your members?**
> **You lust and do not have. You murder and covet
> and cannot obtain. You fight and war. Yet you
> do not have because you do not ask.**
> **You ask and do not receive, because you ask
> amiss, that you may spend *it* on your pleasures.**
> **(James 4:1-3 NKJV)**

Fussing is the fighting and war that the apostle James writes about. It is an internal struggle. It is an external explosion. Each of us has a battle going on within our souls. It is a battle of good and evil; of right and wrong; selfishness and unselfishness. When the battle within is not controlled, then fussing with others is how the conflict is manifested. Now, don't miss this. Our families, our friends, our co-workers, our acquaintances, the stranger in the market place become the battleground for the war raging within us. Or, *[now watch this!]* we become the battleground for a war raging within someone's heart who engages us in conversation.

If we interpret the Epistle of James passage above, from the larger context, we see that the author is dealing with "wisdom" and how to use it. He has shown in the first three chapters of his epistle what real wisdom is. Now, in chapter four the apostle explains that futile, selfish, covetous fussing and fighting is not derived from heaven sent inspiration, but rather enters the scene from the realm of the Evil One and his demons.

> **"Who is wise and understanding among you? Let him show by good conduct *that* his works *are done* in the meekness of wisdom. But if you have bitter envy and self-seeking in your hearts, do not boast and lie against the truth. This wisdom does not descend from above, but is earthly, sensual, demonic. For where envy and self-seeking *exist*, confusion and every evil thing *are* there. (James 3:13-16).**

His reasoning leads us to conclude that <u>fussing is destructive to our lives</u>. And, to continue fussing, fighting and warring is futile. The parties in a fuss will only experience futility unless they can begin to reason with each other. **If one person in the fuss is unreasonable then the fuss is totally futile, and may continue to escalate until a desire and sense of reconciliation prevails from both parties.** Listen to this wisdom:

> *We need to feel the impact of these same truths as James describes situations that are only too true in churches today. The fights and quarrels that James observed characterize the life of the body of Christ and seriously hamper the effective communication of the gospel. Outsiders who look to*

13

the church as a place of solace and salvation often find it is full of strife and danger. We desperately need God's wisdom in our churches.[1]
- Life Application Bible Commentary – James.

What makes a fuss valuable or futile?

Is there any good in a fuss? Sometimes! If a fuss is about eternal, ethical, and/or moral issues, then certainly a healthy fuss or debate will yield good fruit. There can be good, if one of the fussing parties has wisdom enough to discern what the fuss is about, and say, "Wait a minute, let us ask a question – What is the real issue here?" At that point the peace maker should do two things -

1. Take some deep breaths and,

2. Mentally backup and discern what is going on.

"The discretion of a man makes him slow to anger, And his glory is to overlook a transgression" **(Proverbs 19:11).**

I have learned to say when faced with a fuss: "I have to think about this!" The sooner the better. Sometimes I say it to the one who is about to be on the other end of the fuss. Sometimes I simply say it to myself.

---

[1] Bruce B. Barton, *Life Application Bible Commentary: James.* The Livingstone Corporation. 1992 p. 87.

Beyond the discernment, the wise one, in an argument will find a way to state in a positive way what the fuss is about and get agreement from the other party. I searched for a principle for forty years that I could use to help me with this awful action of fussing. My wife and I asked, "Why can there NOT be some kind of trigger to pull or some kind of 'warning light' that shines in the brain when faced with an oncoming fuss?"

RHEMA WORD . . .

A Rhema word is a special word from Scripture. It is a truth, a principle, an insight that God reveals to a person in the midst of a crisis. It gives one the sense that they can face whatever challenge is present and do so with integrity, honesty, and victory.

Through many painful experiences of fussing with church leaders, and market place people, I failed to know how to prevent a fuss. But after much prayer a few years ago, and frustrated that I was "trapped again" into a futile fuss, God showed this powerful verse to me. I could almost hear God my heavenly father saying: "Fuss, fuss, fuss, that's all I ever hear!" And, our Heavenly Father, the All-wise and All-knowing Creator of the universe DOES have an answer for us. The scripture God showed me is truly a *"rhema"* word. And this is the powerful principle my

15

Heavenly Father gave me: (DISCRETION WILL KEEP YOU OUT OF A FUSS!)

"Rhema" is a Greek word which means basically "the subject matter of that which is spoken ' or written." According to Strong's concordance the word "rhema" is used in the Bible approximately seventy times (#4487).[2] Matthew used the word in the following verse: **"But He answered and said, "It is written, Man shall not live by bread alone, but by every word that proceeds out of the mouth of God." (Matthew 4:4 NKJV)**

Peter received a special "rhema" word from Christ during his temptation to deny Jesus: **'And Peter remembered the word of Jesus, who had said to him, "Before the rooster crows, you will deny Me three times." So, he went out and wept bitterly.' (Matthew 26:75 NKJV)**

A.T. Robertson says, "Rhema brings out the single item rather than the whole content."[3]

---

[2] James Strong, *Strong's Concordance;* The National Foundation for Christian Education, Marshallton, DE., p. 63.

[3] A.T. Robertson, Word Pictures in the New Testament, Broadman Press: Nashville, TN., 1930.

"Rhema" is one of three Greek words that can be used for our English communication of "word." The other two are: "logos" which means the whole word like the Bible or even a title of our Lord Jesus; and "hanoma" which means a single word. Rhema has to do with the idea that someone, even God, saying, "May I have a word with you?" or "I have a word FOR you." When someone says that, it does not usually mean the sum total of just one word. The Bible contains words of Pharaohs, Kings, Pharisees, Herodians, Apostles, and Sadducees. Those words are true in the sense that the writer of the Bible quotes them accurately, but they are not always "the" truth. But the Bible is the Word of God, all of it and I believe every word of it. So, when we need help with a crisis or problem or in a fuss, we need a *"rhema"* word from the Bible primarily. An example of this is in the book of Jonah when God says to the prophet, "Go to Nineveh." That is God's "rhema" word for Jonah. When you read the Bible and God speaks to you about your situation, then, that is God's "rhema" word to you.

God calls us to discipleship as followers of Christ. To be Christ-like we hear the call to "die to self" through such passages of Scripture found in the Epistle to the Galatians and the Gospel of Luke.

17

*"I have been crucified with Christ; it is no longer I
who live, but Christ lives in me; and the life which
I now live in the flesh I live by faith in the Son of
God, who loved me and gave Himself for me.
"I do not set aside the grace of God; for if
righteousness comes through the law, then Christ
died in vain." (Galatians 2:20-21)*

*"Then He said to them all, "If anyone desires to
come after Me, let him deny himself, and take up
his cross daily, and follow Me." (Luke 9:23)*

Taking up our cross is difficult. Taking up our cross means
we choose to die (not physically, but spiritually). We place
ourselves, by faith on "the cross" in order to put to death our
sinful desires, our wrongful habits, our unGodly attitudes
and anything that keeps us from being righteous (in right
standing with God). So, when we are tempted to commit any
sin, including sinful fussing, we must make certain, USING
DISCRETION, we are on the cross and dying to selfish
inclinations, persuasions, and motivations.

Sometimes we get into an argument or fussing situation
which is totally surprising to us. We come to a place in
conversations with others and have no idea that THEY are
struggling with emotional things. We become a sounding
board, or a target for their anger, or simply a place where
they can dump their pain. John Ortberg says, "Every once in

18

a while, somebody's 'AS-IS' (emphasis mine) tag becomes high profile."[4] He adds that when something that shocks us or surprises people, "the general public response is, 'Can you believe it? And they seemed so NORMAL?' As if you and I, of course, would be incapable of such behavior."[5] We will learn in this book how we can not only deal with the things that cause us to fuss with others, but also how we can handle the fussing aimed at us, whether we deserve it or not.

Fussing is the outgrowth of discontentment in someone's heart and life. It spills over into others and a fuss begins to brew. The Bible says: *"There is one who speaks like the piercings of a sword, but the tongue of the wise promotes health."* **Proverbs 12:18 (NKJV)** The old adage, "Sticks and stones may break my bones, but words will never harm me" is simply NOT true. Words hurt! Words can destroy! We can use our tongue as a fire to encourage or discourage; to warm or burn up. Our words can be futile, sometimes fatal!

---

[4] John Ortberg, *Everybody's Normal TILL You Get to Know Them*, Zondervan, 2003, p17.
[5] Ibid

People use:

- Reckless Words, "Why don't you go back to where you came from?" Or, "Why don't you go and play on an active runway?" Or, "Did you steal my …?"

- Careless Words, "You can't do that." Or, "I don't care what you think."

- Hurtful Words, "You idiot!" Or "You're a loser."

- Piercing Words, "I hate you." "You will never amount to anything." "You can't do anything right." "Pick up your feet clumsy."

- Shameful Words, (Words I will not use in this book, but you have heard them – the expletives like Hollywood uses, or MTV, or even now heard on primetime TV, talk radio shows, or read on Facebook and Twitter).

I enjoy the work, writings and ministry of Florence Littauer. Through her ministry of writing, I have been helped to understand my personality better and in turn have helped many others discover some important factors in their life makeup. In *Taking Charge of Your Life*, Littauer writes to a lady who said: "I've never understood why any decent person would abuse anyone . . . Can you give me some understanding of the abuser's reasons?" She replied, "Here is a list of explanations for an abuser's behavior with some information to help you assess the situation:

- The abusive person was likely abused himself as a child.

- The abuser tends to abuse in the same way he was violated. If he was beaten, he beats. If he was sexually molested, he molests. If he was verbally abused, he degrades and insults.

Fussing, fighting and warring are: "futile."

- The abuse is usually compulsive behavior, so good intentions, vows, prayers of repentance, and even threats of jail won't necessarily keep him from repeating the offense.

- The abuse probably won't just stop because he is getting older or going to church more. When I ask many women why they allowed the abuse to go on, they tell me they thought their husband would see the error of his ways and change. Seldom is this true.

- The abuser may not see what he's doing as abusive. If he lived with abuse growing up, it seems natural to him. He has no doubt rationalized his behavior as necessary to keep the family under control.

- Power and control are the major motivations for abuse. The abuser, a victim himself, is scared to death he will lose control.[6]

Littauer is right on. The last statement she makes to the lady speaks of power and control. The bottom line as I see it — every person who has a problem with control and authority, power and "being in charge" can only find help through a personal relationship with the Creator, Jesus Christ. This is paramount in the Christian faith. We call it the LORDSHIP OF CHRIST.

Unless a person, with or without OCB (obsessive compulsive behavior), controlled by the need to be in control, or docile and has a "doormat self-image," finds satisfaction, peace and harmony in life through this personal

---

[6] Florence Littauer. Fleming Revell, Grand Rapids, MN. 1999, pp. 126-27.

relationship with Jesus, he will ultimately, always, finally fail.

Fussing is futile because it damages relationships.
Fussing might involve a parent who is not content with a disobedient teenager and says: "Why can't you keep your room clean?" A clean room might be the ticket for the parent's contentment. Yet, the unkempt room is the shortcut to starting a divisive discussion, because from the youth's viewpoint, it may not matter. Then the fuss leads to more rebellion and hurt feelings. A dirty room usually is just the surface evidence of something deeper going on in a relationship. It could reveal a lack of honor to the parent. Or, it could be a disdain for authority. It could reveal the parent's lack of ability to build a loving relationship with the teen.

The challenge of a fuss might be a discontented employer who remarks to the habitually tardy employee: "Why can't you be on time?" Promptness makes for peace in the heart of the employer, yet in the employee's life there may be extenuating circumstances that he has just failed to communicate or is afraid to lay out for his boss, for the fear of being fired. That lack of communication results in conflict.

Both the employee and the employer are right to ask the question, "Who dies to self?" But, to avoid the fuss, a deeper conversation needs to take place. (See and apply addendum). In that dialog each would find the driving issue that can be dealt with and a solution so as to make and/or preserve a harmonious relationship.

Dialog is when both parties can express themselves to the end that there is an ethical and moral synthesis. In the addendum, I have placed a technique I learned from Dr. Rod Marshall, the president and CEO of Alabama Baptist Children's Home and Family Services. He was leading a Pastor and Spouse Marriage Retreat. In his handout he shared a way for couples to communicate in order to avoid arguments, thus preventing a climate of anger and negative attitudes. It was part of "The Prevention and Relationship Enhancement Program" he was teaching. I have called it the 10/5/10/5 tool as I use a modified version of it. Dr. Marshall dubs it *"The Speaker/Listener Technique: One Way to*

Enact James 1:9."[7] It is also a way for a couple who once was madly in love with each other, but now find themselves warring with each other, to regain a sense of "oneness." The idea is for the first speaker to share for ten minutes the burden or problem causing the conflict with the other, but not "go on and on" and stop in order for the listener to give a paraphrase of what was heard. Then the Listener paraphrases for five minutes what was heard, without rebuttal, all the while focusing on the speaker's words. This word construct does not presume that HE goes first! Then it is reversed. The Speaker always "has the floor!" Amos the prophet asks the question every couple needs to face: "Can two walk together unless they are in agreement?" **(Amos 3:3)** This is a good application of the "dying to self" aspect of this book.

Fussing over LOSS is futile. LOSS causes or brings about hurt, anger, regret, guilt and ultimately more fussing. We cannot change the past. We cannot change the unchangeable. Only God can do that. We can't "unshell corn" or "unskin fish." The very prospect of losing

---

[7]https://www.prepinc.com/Content/CURRICULA/Christian-PREP.htm

something valuable creates an atmosphere for a fuss. Some folks "skin" others "alive" when they experience loss. There is pain in an injured or lost relationship as we have already seen. Beyond the pain over something lost, if there is a fuss over the loss, ongoing actions and reactions toward self and/or others fuel the fuss. Many marriages end up in divorce especially because of the fussing that ensues when the couple loses a child in death.

Even the prospect of a loss can and/or might create great pain. A garage full of "keepsakes" or junk can produce a fuss between spouses and siblings. Partners in a business may have great conflict over "bottom line." And in tons of other relationships conflict shows its ugly head, many times over minor bumps and lane changes on the highway of life. As I was approaching retirement years, I was fighting the inevitable FUSS, mostly with myself, over things accumulated for forty-five plus years. My precious wife was so understanding, and has continued to tolerate my collections, which most are still in boxes "in the garage." I'm working on it slowly.

In all these types of conflict feelings come out! Desires and wants take control! The truth about who is Lord of Life is revealed. The one with a possessive spirit drives the fuss as much as the one who thinks the conflict has simple solutions.

Losing valuable time in life by fussing is futile. In another view of the greater context of the passage in James, we see that life is "like a vapor," here for a moment, then GONE! That alone ought to motivate us to NOT waste our time fussing. Of all people who fuss, those in business, should take note that time is money; and those managing a family should see the value of using their valuable time together can be spent in a more honorable way. So, therefore they ought to be experts in the area of conflict resolution. In that way all profit.

We can find so much more to do – important tasks, important things, and important destinations for a short life. We need to see people as the important creation they are and respect their uniqueness. Simply fussing about things is futile. When loss is experienced; fussing about it may have a place momentarily. However, fussing over material things like jewelry it is totally futile. However, in some cases like character, it is essential to a process of civil action against the perpetrator. Proper and honest legal action leads to justice.

When a person decides to curtail a fuss or simply overlook a matter, he is practicing the concept of "dying to self." Selfless living is a virtue. It is huge in building one's world view and learning to get along with people. The Bible says: *"It is honorable for a man to stop striving, Since any fool can start a quarrel."* **Proverbs 20:3 (NKJV)**

Getting along does not mean ignoring someone. Did you know that just simply ignoring someone is a form of hate? We go up and down store aisles, (now folks up north listen carefully – wait it is happening in Alabama and Georgia now, OH MY! We meet people and never make eye contact, nor smile, nor say any sort of greeting to them – we just ignore them. What kind of goodness is in that? Could we not spare at least a simple, "Hi!" I make sure I greet everyone, with a "Hello Neighbor."

Now, here is a bit of gleaned wisdom from Life Application Bible Commentary. The emphasis is mine.

> When you engage someone in a discussion of matters of faith, you will find out fairly quickly whether that person is truly interested in what you have to say or only interested in arguing. If the person is interested, take as much time and effort as you can in giving him or her

answers and information. If the person merely wants a debate, don't oblige. **It is pointless to give intellectual responses to issues of the heart**. The real battleground for that person is not in the mind but in the heart. Until the person has an open heart, as well as an open mind, intellectual discussions will likely only serve to harden his or her disbelief. Save your breath . . . and wait until God prepares the heart.[8]

Well said. In stronger words, "Why should we spend valuable time in fussing about something that has very little value. Move on! Press toward the higher goal and the winnable issues that are afforded to every person in the world. Or, at least commit that time to understanding the individual involved in the fuss. The Apostle Paul said it right, "Redeem the time!"

If we obey Ephesians 4:29-32 and 5:2, which say,

> *"Let no corrupt communication proceed out of your mouth, but what is good for necessary edification, that it may impart grace to the hearers. And do not grieve the Holy Spirit of God by whom*

---

[8]*Life Application Bible Commentary: Luke*, Tyndale, Wheaton, 1991 .

you were sealed for the day of redemption. Let all
bitterness, wrath, anger, clamor, and evil speaking
be put away from you, with all malice. And be
kind to one another, tenderhearted, forgiving one
another, even as God in Christ forgave you.
And walk in love as Christ also has loved us and
given Himself for us, an offering and a sacrifice to
God for a sweet-smelling aroma.

then, we are going to be less likely to get into a "futile fuss"
and we will also be displaying the spiritual maturity to others
that will in turn help them avoid futile fussing.

"A new commandment I give to you, that you love one
another; as I have loved you, that you also love one
another. By this all will know that you are My disciples, if
you have love for one another." **(John 13: 34-35 NKJV)**

While writing the first edition of this book, Patricia and I had
the opportunity to take a vacation to Alaska – our first
extended vacation in many, many years. We spent three days
in Anchorage before boarding our cruise ship. After we left
port, Patricia and I learned something at a seminar about the
TOXINS in our body. We learned that we fill our bodies
with TOXINS – from hair spray, to cleaning supplies, to
home maintenance (gasoline fumes, paint, etc.), to HVAC
units, to the very food we eat, every day. Toxins are not just
found in products we use that invade our bodies. We can

30

find toxins in people that attack our minds, our spirits, our attitudes, our whole way of life. I have personally through fifty plus years of ministry had my share of "toxic people" and/or inordinate individuals. Some people just pick us for the purpose of being obnoxious. Sometimes they become friends and dependable co-workers in spite of the beginning relationship.

In that regard, we do hear the word "toxic" in the business world. When related to a person or an atmosphere of unhealthiness, then we need to avoid or be rid of such, or those toxic words and attitudes will destroy us. There are toxic persons in the workplace who drain the energy, dim the vision, and eventually, if neglected, destroy the very business that pays their salary and benefits.

There are toxic Christians within the church. There are toxic members within a family. There are toxic members in State Houses, in Congress, in the Courts, and in the Executive branch of government. Some countries are filled with toxic citizens. I will deal more intently and specifically with this toward the end of the book.

In our bodies (and the principle holds in business, church and government) the fatty cells build walls around the toxins. The more we eat and the more we reduce our exercise, the shorter is the path to a sick body. It is futile to try to lose weight apart from breaking the water wall around the acidic fat. The "spiritual" fatty wall <u>is an attitude of SELF and SIN</u>, protecting the toxins in relationships, and communication, which in turn makes it futile to try living for God unless we break down this "fatty wall" in our soul. Therefore, we need cleansing.

<u>Fussing is futile when the lasting result is anger and especially if we let anger take us to the bottomless pit of bitterness.</u> Anger is a natural emotion for both the creature and the Creator. Many a pastor and employee lost his job over the expression of this emotion. The problem is usually anger out of control or the person who sees or receives the anger does not understand the real purpose of anger. God shows anger. God tells us to "be angry but do not sin." Many think that any form of anger is sin. If that is true then Christ Himself sinned against the Father. And, that is just not the case, because Christ is sinless. Let me illustrate.

Let's say a Christian deacon is walking down the street and just ahead of him are two boys and a girl bullying a smaller child. He begins to recognize that they are not just playing around, but rather the smaller person is really being hurt. He gets angry at this SIN taking place. In a rushing sprint he gets on the scene and begins to pull the boys and girl away from this smaller child telling them to stop and leave this child alone. He rescues the child from an evil act.

If the deacon had ignored this by refusing to "get angry" he would have supported the abusers. If he just got angry without doing something about it, he would also be guilty of "knowing to good and not doing it" which the Bible calls sin! If he "stays" angry - then he sins because his anger has turned to malice or to bitterness and will cause him to act inappropriately to others.

Psychology Today published an online article: **"Anger, Rage and Pathological Embitterment: What Motivates Mass Murders?"** in which Stephen A. Diamond wrote:

> "The violence epidemic (and there surely is one today, despite what evolutionary psychologist Steven Pinker naively says in his newest book) is really a rage epidemic. It is a new and pernicious form of violence arising in part from a postmodern loss of meaning, power, significance and conscious

relationship with the *daimonic*. We frail humans are prone to feeling hurt. And when we feel hurt, we are prone to feeling angry. If we deny this anger, dismiss it, deem it merely destructive, uncivilized and therefore, evil, fail to embrace and provide it some positive outlet, it will eventually become exactly that. But if we acknowledge it, recognize it, find ways to constructively express it, anger, rather than becoming toxic or pathological rage, resentment or embitterment, can be empowering and positive. When individuals cannot manage their anger constructively, when it begins turning into pathological embitterment, depression, irritability, temper tantrums or manic rage, professional help is required.[9]

Anger can help us change things that are wrong. Anger will help us cope with things we can't change. In that I mean, we will learn to adjust to those "unchangeables" so that we can function in life. It gives us a chance to process those things so that perhaps later we can respond effectively. What are some of those unchangeables? Here is a short list:

- How others "think" of him / her / us

- Challenge in social skills

- Handicaps

- The misuse of natural resources

---

[9] https://www.psychologytoday.com/blog/evil-deeds/201110/anger-rage-and-pathological-embitterment-what-motivates-mass-murders

- The poverty that is worldwide

- The trafficking of women, girls and boys into human slavery

All of these things can lead us into frustration. Sometimes this frustration leads us into greater anxiety which leads to anger. Anger must be controlled or we fuss, fuss, fuss.

> *So then, my beloved brethren, let every man be swift to hear, slow to speak, slow to wrath; for the wrath of man does not produce the righteousness of God. James 1:19-20 (NKJV)*

> *"A worthless person, a wicked man, Walks with a perverse mouth; He winks with his eyes, He shuffles his feet, He points with his fingers; Perversity is in his heart, He devises evil continually, He sows discord." (Proverbs 6:12-14 NKJV)*

The Mayo Clinic, an internationally known source for health, placed on their web site ten tips to tame anger's driving force – our temper. The article is very helpful and begins with the word – "Keeping your temper in check can be challenging." The Mayo Clinic Staff pooled their efforts and knowledge to give us the following: "Anger is a normal and even healthy emotion — but it's important to deal with it in a positive way. Uncontrolled anger can take a toll on both your health and your relationships." The Ten Anger Management Tips are (without the annotation):

1. **Think before you speak**
2. **Once you're calm, express [in words] your anger**
3. **Get some exercise**
4. **Take a timeout**
5. **Identify possible solutions**
6. **Stick with 'I' statements**
7. **Don't hold a grudge**
8. **Use humor to release tension**
9. **Practice relaxation skills**
10. **Know when to seek help.**[10]

The next chapter will help us begin to take a stand in the midst of fussing. We will also see how it is important to die to self. That is:

The challenge of dying to self and knowing when to stand.

---

[10] http://www.mayoclinic.org/healthy-living/adult-health/in-depth/anger-management/art-20045434?pg=2

Chapter 2

Dying to a Futile Experience

In a fuss, who dies to self? Either or both! All across the nation in our Sunday Schools and in our Youth groups are leaders who face week after week someone who needs ministry because a fuss is brewing at home, at school, in the streets, on the playground. Hopefully, this book will provide some insight on how fussing can be curtailed and solutions found.

Believers, of all people, ought to do everything possible to reduce the friction and the fussing within the church. It should be a top priority of the Christian to learn how to resolve conflict, avoid fussing and pass that secret on to others. This one action will influence families, businesses and the world at large. The person who is willing to deny oneself of being "right" or "justified" can win in the long run. The patience that comes from that kind of discipline will yield its perfect fruit as the fuss transforms into a conversation and then into a richer experience of dialog.

> *"You also be patient. Establish your hearts, for the coming of the Lord is at hand. (James 5:8)*

The moment, the very moment that a fuss begins, the stronger Christian ought to employ patient understanding. Then with the same assurance that Christ will return some day to straighten out every conflict, a believer should speak words of healing from an established heart, to those in a crisis. Yes, I am suggesting that we live with a great expectation of Christ coming again! We can bring eternity and our actions together to get a clearer perspective and gain Godly wisdom by looking at what the Apostle Paul said to the Romans:

> *"But... God, ... "will render to each one according to his deeds": eternal life to those who by patient continuance in doing good seek for glory, honor, and immortality. (Romans 2:7)*

In eternity much of what we fuss about will be useless. Even in the here and now much of our fussing is not worthy of a "win" or a battle worth pursuing. You and I have family members who, EVERY DAY they live must WIN every challenge, every contention, every disagreement, every battle, whether it is in the game of life or just simply playing games in life. Some battles are not worth the fallout to "win" and certainly every game cannot be won. A friend once told me as we were playing table "games" – it all goes back in the box when we are finished playing. We must answer for our deeds someday – although salvation is sealed, our works will be judged. Through the actions of everyday living, we ought to seek glory and honor for our immortal King.

> *"And not only that, but we also glory in tribulations, knowing that tribulation produces perseverance"* *(Romans 5:3; 2:7)*

> *". . . that you do not become sluggish, but imitate those who through faith and patience inherit the promises."* *(Hebrews 6:12)*

When we fuss continually with someone, we are forgetting that we are imitators of those who have gone on before us in victory. We have much to inherit THERE and most of the time we do not have to worry about "stuff" HERE.

The Anchorage Daily News ran a cartoon by Patrick McDonnell called "Mutts." The characters are a dog and a cat. The pair discovers a treasure chest. The cat asks, "What treasures could be in that chest?' The next frame shows the picture cloud over the dog with a bone and the cat's picture cloud shows a sock. The third and final frame shows the dog and cat on top of the treasure chest fussing, saying to each other, "It's MINE!"[11] We act like this dog and cat when we fuss. We claim things that don't belong to us. We imagine things that may or may not be true. And, we ruin relationships because we act selfishly.

Who dies? Who stands?

I've known brothers who have lived side by side since leaving their parents' home and had not spoken to each other for thirty years due to a fuss. The brothers argued over a fence between their properties. When I became their pastor, the fence was nearly gone – the wire was rusty and weak; the posts were rotten and falling over, yet the hurt, bitterness and pain was very much alive. The fuss was futile.

A good example of someone taking a stand in a fuss is the Olympian runner, Eric Liddell of Scotland. Liddell was a devout Christian and refused to enter the final competition when he learned that it would happen on Sunday. Because of his devotion to Christ and worship on Sunday, he took a stand, virtually costing him the gold medal. Yet, he went on

---

[11] Patrick McDonnell, *Anchorage Daily News.* August 21, 2013, p. B-12.

to run the 400 meters race, beyond Sunday, won it and became a true Olympian hero.[12]

Another example I observed recently was when a lady, noted for her verboseness, entered the room and after only one person finished what "he" was saying, she began to tell her "stories." She ranted on about all the wonderful things she was doing, barely taking a breath. The host and hostess showed kindness, flexibility, and understanding. While there was no "stand" against her rudeness, the couple stood with their Christian character intact. For, there could have been a big fuss.

Still another true-life story was told to us on that trip to Alaska. On a tour of Anchorage, the trolley driver told us about a huge fuss that happened during Easter Week, 1964. The local high school had scheduled a basketball tournament on Good Friday. Some of the Catholic moms argued (or at best "stood their ground") and told the school authorities that their families would be in Mass on Friday. How gutsy is that? The school changed the date!

---

[12] http://www.historymakers.info/inspirational-christians/eric-liddell.html

On that Good Friday the second largest recorded earthquake hit Anchorage, flattening the school building where the High School Tournament had been scheduled. What a miracle from a fuss! What a great story of someone taking a stand in a fuss!

Elijah is a good Biblical model of someone taking a stand. As the fiery prophet of God, Elijah stood against wicked King Ahab and the "more wicked" Queen Jezebel. The display of God's power in taking this stand is recorded in 1 Kings 18. This true story of a great man clearly encourages the believer in Christ to take a stand for what is just and right.

In Virginia recently, moms took a stand against an ungodly school board and told that school board that their children were not going to be taught Critical Race Theory, which is one of the biggest lies ever perpetrated upon our culture and to our children. They won. They have a new governor who has promised to do away with such garbage in the classroom.

In "Grandparents' Brag Board," a humorous section of *Mature Living*, Betty Britt of Baton Rouge, Louisiana, tells about her four year old grandson, Chase who had a visit with a doctor to get a booster shot before his first day in kindergarten. She writes, "Naturally, he was quite upset about this. When he finally stopped sobbing, he announced, "I'm not going to college if I have to get another shot!" "[13] Chase took a stand! Some folks make immature stands. Chase's stand is funny and perfect for his age. However, adults who take a stand without complete knowledge of a situation can be totally embarrassed and possibly not taken seriously in future fusses.

The Bible says, *"Therefore, let us pursue the things which make for peace and the things which one may edify another."* **Romans 14:19 (NKJV)** We must take specific action in order to do that. Sometimes it requires the dying to self. To edify another is to build him up, not tear down an individual's character and confidence. Paul follows that with, *"Now may the God of patience and comfort grant you to be like-minded toward one another, according to Christ Jesus."* **Romans 15:5 (NKJV) The** author of Wisdom Literature in the Old Testament gives us this: *"He who passes by and meddles in a quarrel not his own Is like one who takes a dog by the ears."* **Proverbs 26:17 (NKJV)** In addition to that bit of wisdom, Paul adds: *"But if you bite*

---

[13] *Mature Living*, January 2008; LifeWay Press, Nashville, TN; p.8.

and devour one another, beware lest you be consumed by one another!" **Galatians 5:15 (NKJV)**

Who Dies? Who Stands?

The fuss over keepsakes may come at the death of the last parent and the children have to decide what to do with the "stuff." Some parents leave huge sums of money and large tracts of real estate to their offspring. Usually, those things can be easily handled. But, what about: "Mother's quilt?" or, "Daddy's watch"? It can be something as small as a piece of costume jewelry. What about someone losing a piece of jewelry. Blaming someone else for "stealing it" can create much strife and argument.

Other folks lose their integrity and respect due to poor choices. A huge fuss ensues over character. To either loser the loss is valuable and worth fighting for. If a person is confronted then the "accusation" has generated a fuss. In the case of the lost jewelry, it may be found and a false accusation, say by a parent to a child, can have lasting repercussions. Trust has to be rebuilt. In the case of character, say by a teenage girl who was molested by a

family member, the permanent damage will always be her
challenge.

This book is about helping you and me cleanse our lives of
at least ONE toxin – "fussing" – so that we can live healthier
and more fruitful lives. Just imagine a business or church,
or our government getting rid of the fussing activity. How
much more productive and how much richer our lives would
be!

Toxic tongues are a result of toxic attitudes. Toxic attitudes
result from toxic beliefs. Toxic beliefs are accumulated
when a person does not have a personal relationship with
God through Jesus Christ.

> **"So speak and so do as those who will be judged
> by the law of liberty. For judgment is without
> mercy to the one who has shown no mercy.
> Mercy triumphs over judgment."
> (James 2:12-13 NKJV)**

We will deal with how to have victory over these issues later
in this book in the chapter on forgiveness. Suffice it to say
now in the words of Peter the Apostle:

> **"Finally, all of *you* be of one mind, having
> compassion for one another; love as brothers, *be*
> tenderhearted, *be* courteous; not returning evil
> for evil or reviling for reviling, but on the**

45

contrary blessing, knowing that you were called
to this, that you may inherit a blessing."
(1 Peter 3:8-9)

"Hatred stirs up strife, But love covers all sins."
 (Proverbs 10:12 NKJV)

Who dies? Who stands?

The challenge of dying to self
and knowing when to stand.

Chapter 3

The Friction of a Fuss

(FIGHT)

Sometimes we argue with ourselves. We fight our conscience to the point of exhaustion. Sometimes we make a decision that spins us into conflict, and others are quickly drawn into it. Most people (unless trained in Spiritual warfare – addressed briefly throughout this book) are oblivious to the Biblical passages that teach how to

> ➤ NOT create conflict

> ➤ resolve conflict and,

> ➤ use alternative actions in dealing with conflict.

Psalm 102 - 103 is a great place to check our attitude so that we might prevent becoming embroiled in a great fuss. These two Psalms help us discern whether we want to mope in the desert with owls and pelicans or rise above our circumstances as eagles and master fussing. You see, God, the Everlasting God, your Creator hears your groans and sees your dilemma when you are caught in a fuss with seemingly no way out. The Psalmist gives us the answer in the context of these two chapters. **One,** we need to know that God is listening and knows. **Two,** God wants us to pray and talk to Him, then He will provide counsel for us. **Three,** we learn to depend on Him, trusting Him to take care of the concerns when we cannot help ourselves. **Fourth,** we move to the attitude of praise as we declare, *"Bless the Lord O' my soul!"* Then, we can see all the benefits that God provides. Read these two chapters carefully.

I chopped my left thumb and screamed in pain.

I had an experience likened to Christians fussing in spite of the Scriptural injunction against it. But, no one was listening, except God, because I was by myself in the backyard of my home place, visiting my widowed mother. I planned to do some chores for her. It was an early Fall Day, still rather warm. I was getting my mother ready for the cold Winter days ahead. I took the liberty to cut some "kindlin' " for her to use in her kitchen stove. My brothers had bought a truck load of scrap lumber in short pieces. I tuned the radio to WJJC – the local station which I grew up with. Two talk show hosts were sharing stories back and forth. I got the hatchet, a chopping block and used an empty five-gallon bucket, turned upside down, to sit on. I grabbed a cardboard box for the chopped wood. As I listened, one of the radio disc jockeys asked his co-host if he had heard about the man who attended his own funeral. "No" was the reply. The first DJ went on to explain what happened. I was chopping away, halfway listening, but really tuned in when the DJ said the funeral was conducted by a Baptist preacher. That got my full attention! Then the clincher came – now mind you, I'm still chopping blocks for kindling, with a sharp blade – when the DJ said, "The man chose *I Did it My Way* by 'ole Blue Eyes!"[14]

---

[14]http://en.wikipedia.org/wiki/My_Way:_The_Best_of_Frank_Sinatra (Comment: As a conservative Southern Baptist for over 51 years I believe strongly that we need to be careful about the music we use in ANY service we render for church members or the public at large. Our good name is at stake if we give credence to worldly entertainers.)

That did it for me! I was disturbed to say the least (See comment in footnote one page back). With hatchet falling, I began to fuss angrily with the DJ (of course he could not hear me!) saying, "NO WAY! NO WAY! Not in my church! As pastor I'd never let that happen in my Baptist church!" I chopped my left thumb and screamed in pain. I realized what I had done, grabbed it and ran for help. I only cut off a small portion of the left side of my thumb, but I sure learned a serious lesson. Fussing is futile and dangerous. Friction in a fuss increases the futility and the pain. No wonder the writer of Proverbs says:

"The discretion of a man makes him slow to anger, And his glory is to overlook a transgression." **(Proverbs 19:11 NKJV)**

If I had simply smiled at the story and overlooked the bad judgment of some pastor's poor funeral planning, I would not have chopped my thumb. I should have practiced this principle*: "Cease from anger, and forsake wrath; Do not fret--it only causes harm."* **Psalm 37:8 (NKJV)**

Boy! Does it! And also, *"Do not hasten in your spirit to be angry, For anger rests in the bosom of fools."* **Ecclesiastes**

7:9 (NKJV) What a fool I was for letting a simple story ruin a very good day and for responding in such a way as to self-inflict my body!

Further, the writer of wisdom says: *"For as the churning of milk produces butter, And wringing the nose produces blood, So the forcing of wrath produces strife."*
Proverbs 30:33 (NKJV)

And also, *"The beginning of strife is like releasing water; Therefore stop contention before a quarrel starts."*
Proverbs 17:14 (NKJV)

Dam breaks like the Georgia tragedy at Toccoa Falls, and hurricanes like Andrew in south Florida, and Katrina on the Gulf coast; and flooding like we have seen in many states, wreak havoc upon the land and the people around in these areas. Others like the citizens of Colorado who have experienced the destruction of tons and tons of water rushing through their streets, their parks, and their yards – unabated and taking down everything in its path. People with a loose tongue and angry spirit are very destructive. Sometimes it is destructive to themselves as well as others. Now in our day as I write this revision, a Pandemic of Covid 19 has the world in fear and most of it is useless because of lying politicians and medical people who will not be fair and honest about the virus. They cry "Science!" and yet they say nothing almost about natural immunity or how "boosters" actually harm a person's natural immunity. There is a hidden agenda at the expense of freedom, jobs, school children, small businesses, churches and our national morality.

Fussing is the result of strife between two or more parties and fussing destroys relationships when it comes in like a storm and floods our spirit. The Apostle Paul states,

> **"Let us walk properly, as in the day, not in revelry and drunkenness, not in lewdness and lust, not in strife and envy. But put on the Lord Jesus Christ, and make no provision for the flesh, to *fulfill its* lusts." Romans 13:13-14 (NKJV)**

Would you not agree that when we "produce" (show) strife with someone we are performing immaturely, inconsiderately, selfishly and with an unholy countenance, which is less than what God expects from us? If so, would you agree that those times of strife are futile? The only exception is when we strive against immorality and perversion. Strife and fussing erode peace and joy and relationships, like a mighty river which has overrun its banks.

The answer is for a person to have a relationship with the Prince of Peace, Jesus Christ. This oneness with Christ allows Him to take away the carnality and the selfishness and the attitudes that bring about the fight of a fuss. We find in Paul's letter to the Corinthians these words:

". . .for you are still carnal. For where *there are* envy, strife, and divisions among you, are you not carnal and behaving like *mere* men?" 1 Corinthians 3:3 (NKJV)

Someone asked, while filling in a crossword puzzle: "What is a five-letter word that means boomerang?"

The answer: ANGER

And,

"Now these things, brethren, I have figuratively transferred to myself and Apollos for your sakes, that you may learn in us not to think beyond what is written, that none of you may be puffed up on behalf of one against the other. For who makes you differ *from another?* And what do you have that you did not receive? Now if you did indeed receive *it,* why do you boast as if you had not received *it?*" (1 Corinthians 4:6-7 NKJV)

Fuss! Fuss! Fuss!

In Genesis 49:23, Jacob recounts Joseph's battle with various people, including his brothers, Potiphar's wife, and others. He refers to these "enemies" as "archers with malice" who shot their arrows at him. That is the way people treat each other. We shoot each other with arrows of malice hoping to hurt, malign and destroy. Like Joseph, when we face people filled with malice, we need to be strong, maintain our defense with integrity, be flexible enough to hear and understand, and depend upon the God of Abraham, Isaac, and Jacob, who is our Shield, our Rock and Defender.

Hurt and pain, depression and malice come from fussing.

Sometimes we fuss with people either one on one or one with many or group against group. We also fuss with things, over events, time and a person named Murphy (circumstantial frustration). This could be: late for a flight; a flat tire; losing a wallet. For the melancholy person it seems that the proverbial "Murphy" shows up, oh so very often, and creates a situation impregnated with a fuss. Whatever or wherever it is, there will be friction and where there is friction the laws of thermal dynamics demand that there be heat. Where there is emotional heat usually anger results. [I have learned that "Murphy" is just another way of alluding to the Evil One and thus I now refrain from saying, "Murphy did this or that."] My experience with Sinatra's song was really small marbles. It was a minute theological hot button. But there are boulders out there that have national and international consequences. Let's look at some God-sized friction. The friction points described below must be handled with Scripture in order for any person to find victory over them.

1. Debt

Finance and the misuse of money is the cause of most family problems in the United States. Many divorces can be traced to fussing over money or the lack thereof. The average debt of households in the United States is: $90K and the average credit card debt is almost $15,000.

Put on the brakes. Somebody needs to stand against the milieu of attacks on our national economy, starting with the family and going all the way to the Congress and the White House. Issuing mandates for masking and vaccines is not the way to solve this crisis. This kind of "unscientific" and "anti-business" thought only makes for trouble in the economy and destroys the American Dream. Common sense seems to have escaped most of the leadership in our nation. Prudence is still a good word and needs to be utilized.

2. Disease

While we are seeing longer life, in the United States and other places in the world because of great medical discoveries and available health care, many folks still suffer. Much of the suffering causes personal conflict as well as family conflict. Conflict arises in the doctor's office, in the emergency room, in the hospital, and when the patient comes home. Employment is threatened. Some employers refuse to take care of the diseased employee and conflict ensues.

3. Deception

Whether it is a spouse, or business person, a child or a parent, a church leader or church member, a politician or the one being served, when deception is introduced into a relationship, conflict will abound. Fussing fuels the conflict whereby the end is usually less than healthy. Washington D.C. is filled with deception as are all the governments of the world. I challenge anyone to prove otherwise. When the leaders of nations use deception as easily as they do their pens and phones the fallout is horrendous, since most citizens will justify the same sin in their own dealings with others. The rationale is: "If it works for the government it works for me."

4. Disappointment

All of us have experienced disappointment in life. Whatever relationship we have with another human being we must always be prepared for disappointment. We don't expect disappointment in the sense that we set up ourselves or the other person for failure, but simply because none of us bats a thousand. If we are gracious, kind and courteous then we can handle the disappointment and care for the other person. This action can serve to prevent fussing and ultimately preserve the relationship. We disappoint others. When we do, we need to assume the right attitude and responsibility to correct it if possible. Then we need to move on to improving the relationship.

5. <u>Despair</u>

Despair is the fruit of disappointment and frustration. It needs to be curtailed the moment it is recognized. Despair is a tool that will destroy a person spiritually, emotionally, morally and physically. While a fuss may not ever occur as a result of despair, one needs to see that when despair is a part of daily life, it is time to go deeper into the problem and root out the cause of that despair. Usually, a fuss has driven a person to despair. Words hurt. And words sometimes determine how a person reacts to a situation.

6. **Demons**

There is not a demon behind every Ford, or Toyota or even behind every hedge bush. I think I have seen them on the highway a few times! But demons are real. They are the mini-viceroys of this world, as the Prince and Power of the air seeks to rule and reign in the hearts and lives of humanity. Spiritual Warfare must include Biblical instruction on dealing with demons. It must place major emphasis on who is the real King – Jesus Christ the Lord and only True God. Eternity is at stake. (Galatians 5:20)

Hurt and pain, depression and malice come from fussing. Fussing produces burning friction between relationships. Friction begins small. It is like tapping on my auto brakes. Just a tap will raise the temperature on the disc a little bit. But, if I hold the brake pedal down longer, the temperature is increased and keeps going up until I release the brake pedal. The longer one engages in a fuss, the hotter the fussing parties become.

Friction can be good or bad. It is good for a brake system. It is bad on a piston. It is good for sanding a piece of furniture being restored. It is bad for a finished piece of fine furniture.

In a restaurant the customer who engages a waitress with politeness finds no friction in the momentary relationship. But, if one engages the same waitress with complaint and disgust or disdain then he finds friction and possibly more reasons to complain. Not to mention what might happen to the food! Parents can not only reduce the friction in a fuss but teach children how to avoid and reduce friction in the conversation.

Sometimes when I am fishing, my hook "catches" something that gives the idea that I have a big fish on the line. I work to get it in. Then I see it. There is a wad of fishing line, with hooks and sinkers and twigs, and, some other things that it has collected along the way. However, I think about the other end of the line while the fisherman was using it. Somehow his tackle got caught in a place, maybe helped by a big fish, and he couldn't get it untangled. Here that poor soul is, hoping for a big catch, realizing that nothing is there and he can't get it untangled. Frustrated, and perhaps cussing and fussing he simply cuts it loose. The man on the other end of the line is a picture of many people in everyday life. They get in a tangle with someone, it creates a big fussy wad, and when it is not resolved the way they want it to be, they simply "cut the other person or persons loose."

Yes, there is FRICTION in a FUSS!

Friction is the warning light to respond to . . .

. . .The challenge of dying to self and knowing when to stand.

Chapter 4

Standing in the Midst of Friction

I've never had to go looking for a fight. It seems from boyhood days the fight always found me. I depended on my trusty bicycle to get away from the bullies and take me safely home. Somehow, we learn to avoid the fights in life unless we just love conflict and dissension. I don't. Yet, there have been way too many in my life. Somehow in the adult arena I just didn't have a trusty bike to "get me out of there." Until now! Can you agree?

There are times we simply need to get away from a fuss or a fight, especially if it is really none of our business. We certainly don't want to be busy bodies and meddle in business that we have no stake in. Wisdom teaches us to leave some things alone and some people alone. There are some things that we learn, soon in life hopefully, that are as the military expresses it – "not a hill to die on." Then, on the other hand, there are issues, and matters that matter in which we need to and ought to take a stand on. We even, as Christians, or just good citizens of a free country, need to be ready to stand against evil and evil doers, and be ready to be counted among the winners, willing to make the ultimate sacrifice of giving our life for a cause.

So, briefly let me share with you some principles of taking a stand. The Bible is replete with heroes who took a stand. A quick "slide-show-like" list follows:

1. Abraham with his nephew Lot against a whole city of homosexual immorality
2. Joseph in the house of Pharoah against a seductive woman
3. Moses in Egypt before Pharoah against a tyrannical leader
4. Joshua in Canaan against a multiplicity of pagan nations
5. Samuel against a king who would rather serve himself than the God who called him
6. David the Shepherd before Goliath – a nine-foot-tall giant
7. Elijah before a wicked queen and her equally wicked husband

8. Jeremiah weeping for kings and a rebellious nation

9. All the Minor prophets against their homeland led by wicked leaders

10. John the Baptist against Herod the Great

11. Jesus speaking with the Pharisees

12. The disciples of Christ facing an ungodly Roman Empire led by Caesar and his minions

13. Church leaders of the first, second and third centuries who stood against heresy, and other attacks upon truth and their faith, such as Polycarp, the pastor of the church at Smyrna, martyred in his eighties; and the disciple of Polycarp, named Irenaeus who pastored a church in what is now known as France; and there he refuted heresy of his day, giving his life for the truth

Chuck Swindoll, founding teacher of *Insight of Living*, says about these and other such heroes:

> **In the chaos of competing theories of the early church, criticisms against authentic Scripture, and attacks on the doctrine of Jesus Christ, Christians can rest assured that the essential truths of the faith were entrusted to faithful men who respected the teachings of Christ and the apostles. Not only did they live their lives for this faith, but they were also willing to die for it. They were imperfect in mind and speech, subject to the foibles of all sinful human vessels, and often in need of correction by God's perfect, inerrant**

Word. Yet because they took a stand for the truth, today we are able to read His written Word, the Bible, and worship His living Word, Jesus Christ, with confidence.[15]

After the Bible books were written, Church history records other giants of the faith who faced their culture and declared the truth of God in Christ. Evangelists, missionaries and other people of faith simply presented the Gospel and gave their lives for it. They refused to compromise truth and their faith. Check out www.Christianity.com as a great source for learning about those who have STOOD for the faith. Note this regarding one of our heroes from the 15th century:

Savonarola became one of the great names of his age. Pietro de Medici of Florence was a weak man. Savonarola's allies deposed the ineffectual tyrant and the priest became the city's effective leader, and a gadfly in the side of the corrupt Renaissance Pope, Alexander VI. He denounced papal iniquity and took political sides against the pope. Worst of all, from the Pope's point of view, he called upon Europe's leaders to dethrone the pontiff.[16]

---

[15] http://www.insight.org/resources/articles/church-history/heros.html?t=church-history

[16] http://www.christianity.com/church/church-history/timeline/1201-1500/savonarolas-interrogation-and-sentence-11629904.html

How did they do? What can we learn from them to help us **STAND** in the midst of a fuss or crisis? Learning from those who have gone before us will help us to stand, when we must in order to NOT compromise our faith nor deny our Lord. The components of a great plan **to stand** include:

> People who take a stand have "character" and it is character that builds a nation NOT Congress.

- Prayer
- Knowing God's word
- Understanding God's purposes
- Employing personality and people skills we observe in people who stay true to the Christian faith
- Realizing that the message may not be accepted but that it needs to be presented regardless of cost
- Calling upon the Holy Spirit to empower and enlighten us
- Putting on the whole armor of God.

When our "fuss" is ethical, morally right, and Biblically correct, then, we need to stand firm, stand strong, and stand together. Dr. Ron Johnson, author, speaker and an internationally known consultant, writes in his book *Make a Life: Not Just a Living*, "I believe this lack of a collective ethical backbone is the biggest factor contributing to the breakdown of morals and ethics in our society today."[17] He was alluding to the illustration he just used in his book regarding the unethical and unpatriotic actions of a Roseanne Barr opening of the 1990's baseball season in Jack Murphy Stadium. Barr, known for her nasty ways, showed irreverence and unbecoming gestures as she sang the national anthem, to which America said "enough is enough." This "collective ethical backbone" begins with each individual being willing to "stand" against those things and those people who don't measure up to God's righteousness. As Dr. Johnson explores the values and the ethical thinking of today's America, he quotes James Patterson, chairman of the J. Walter Thompson Company, and Peter Kim, director of research services and customer behavior of the same corporation, who conducted "the most massive in-depth survey of what Americans really believe that has ever been conducted."[18] These researchers wrote: "Americans are

---

[17] Ron Johnson, *Make a Life*, Nashville, TN: Broadman and Holman, p. 82
[18] Ibid, p.83 (Johnson)

making up their own rules and laws . . . We choose which laws of God we believe. There is absolutely no moral consensus in this country, as there was in the fifties and sixties."[19] Does this not sound like the period of the Judges in the Old Testament, when God declared through the writer of Judges, "Every man did that which is right in his own eyes?" There was an absence of moral leadership in those Old Testament days. I certainly believe we are in the same predicament today. The United States of America is destitute in the area of LEADERSHIP. And we face God's judgment because of it.

More recently in our culture we have seen millions of citizens of the United States take a stand against a very anti-American football player who insisted he had the right to "take a knee" and not stand for the national anthem. What kind of parents and schools missed the mark in the life of a young man like that? Where was the training he needed? How can he even justify his actions with the freedom he has and the money he makes and the voice he has to even consider that belittling our flag is the way to be heard. He needs help beyond the NFL kicking him out.

---

[19] Ibid, p83 (Johnson)

That is why this book is a clarion call to you and your family to take a stand when it is morally right to do so. Baby Boomers are passing the baton to Gen-Xers and the Millennials – and it won't happen without a fuss. But all generations need to realize how reducing the conflict in the transition of leadership and power will make for a better world. All generations need those wise leaders who will unswervingly take the stand for truth, justice and mercy. It will be those kinds of leaders who will shape this nation to be and do what is good and healthy. Sometimes our fussing is good. Sometimes we can make a difference. If we are not standing, then fuss is futile and the friction becomes unbearable.

Do you see how fussing hurts? Hurts you? Hurts others? Do you like causing friction between you and others? If NOT -- STOP!

Solomon warned us from his reservoir of wisdom, *"Don't be rash with your mouth."* **Ecclesiastes 5:2 (NKJV)** While writing this chapter, the first time, the diabolical events of Aurora, Colorado, and Sandy Hook, Connecticut were being argued over the airways, discussed in homes and Sunday School classes around the nation. Every talk show host and every news program is trying to hammer out the ethical, moral and political issues surrounding the killing of twelve innocent Americans and the injuring of fifty eight (58) others; twenty-six (26) small children and their teachers. And, as I continue working on this volume the matter has only gotten worse. It seems the White House and the so-called "Lame-stream media" just wait to jump on these incidences in order to promote their biases and the socialistic agenda upon the United States. Each incident is a fuss that moves this world to greater tyranny. Lawyers are fussing over the issues. Pastors are expounding on the topic. The fuss is over guns. That is not even close to the issues.

One such fuss as I write this revision is the Rittenhouse case, where a 17-year-old used a gun in Kenosha, Wisconsin and by self-defense shot and killed two men and injured a third. Papers and internet news are filled with biased reports, many stemming from a lying prosecutor. All the people who were seeking to convict this young man had one purpose:

Do away with our second amendment.

The answer is simple. We have freedom of speech as given in the first amendment. We have the right to bear arms in the second amendment, which protects the first amendment.

The size of the gun does not matter. The "enemy" and the forces that want to harm decent law-abiding citizens now carry larger weapons. What are we to do, revert to a pellet gun or a slingshot? I don't think so. The young man was found NOT GUILTY, truth was revealed, and yet there are still people who are fussing over the issue.

During this "revision" life-changing issues are being discussed and demonized. Lame stream media has since become socialistic media and liberal propaganda, all in the name of "freedom of speech" and yet THEY want to silence the voice of conservatism. Family breakdown, mental illness, poor or non-existent moral teaching, selfishness, wrong choice of role models and hatred are the real issues that ought to be dealt with. Very few are interested in what God thinks about it all. This is the time for people to take a stand for God and for the righteous foundations of the nation. Psalm 11:1 says: "If the foundations be destroyed, what can the righteous do?" People who take a stand have "character" and it is character that builds a nation NOT Congress!

The United States is a republic NOT a democracy. That means it is governed by LAWS enacted by Congress, State Legislatures, County Governments, City Governments and

70

the like. These laws are presented, discussed and voted on in a democratic fashion. It is NOT just a system where "majority" rules. Our capitalistic system is and was founded on Biblical principles. As we watch these principles erode, we also see the fabric of the United States of America becoming weaker and weaker. Our nation, if we follow this trajectory, will become just another insipid nation on the heap of history. So, it will be with businesses and families unless we take this issue of fussing seriously and deal with it in a Biblical way. Most citizens of the United States do not even understand that this is a republic. You don't believe me? Ask the next ten persons what the difference is between the two. My guess is that only one person if that, will be able to answer correctly. Try it today!

"If the foundations be destroyed, what can the righteous do?" **(Psalms 11:1 NKJV)**

Instead of removing guns from law-abiding citizens, our leadership ought to be focused on the list mentioned above. For instance, how well are we dealing with Road Rage; domestic violence; corporate anger; deceit; reverse racism; retaliation? Why are we listening to the voices of Al Sharpton, and the Squad and Lebron James, and BLM?

71

These constitute the root of the problems. Someone taking a gun in a moment of severe depression and fueled by Neo Nazism or radical Islamic theology, and killing precious, innocent people, going about their everyday life, minding their own business is only the symptom of a sickness. The world needs to know that the Word of God and the Gospel of Jesus Christ can cure these evils.

Church folks, known as Christians, have the power to deal with these fusses and the causes. The call is for every Christian to take a STAND, hold fast to the Biblical standards our nation and family were founded upon, and never surrender to the pressure of a degenerate world. It is high time for the remaining BUILDER GENERATION, BOOMERS, BRIDGERS, MILLENIALS, and GEN-Xers to step up, take a stand and regain control of this nation.

Why do people who fuss insist on being right? Is it because of sin? I would say, "YES!" Part of the answer is a thing called sinful pride. Sometimes it is arrogance. At other times it is pure ignorance. Sometimes a person's "world view" (their philosophy- the way they view life), or their ingrained culture can block the truth from their minds. Sometimes those blocks make them claim to know

72

something, when in reality they are limited in resolving a fuss. At times the fussing party may display fear and refuse to open themselves to learn truth.

If we take a stand as I propose within this book, I have to warn you that you might find yourself in danger. What are the dangers of fussing? If you stand, you will be standing against crime, hatred, people who are aligned with evil, and many times political power bases. Let me be clear. WE who live in the United States of America, have the greatest privileges of anyone in the world. Oh, yes, we have crime. We have poverty. We have violence. We have all the makings of a fussing nation. But, we have the best nation (for now) of all the nations of the world, simply because we are still at the core, a Christian nation. One of the problems we have in comparing our nation to other nations is that we keep better records than do most. WE really need to stop comparing nations but rather measure our nation to the Biblical concepts that made this nation pleasing to God in it's founding. Is Yemen tracking ALL their violence? Is Libya taking seriously every incident of crime within her borders? Are Russia and China acknowledging to the world everything that is perpetrated against their nation? Are the nations of the world really opposed to child abuse, and child slavery? So, in light of the fact that we have much wrong reported in the U. S. A. (And, not all of it is), we must STAND.

I highly recommend that you get informed about possessing a firearm. Get the training by a professional that you need for safety and for the use of your weapon. Don't just go out and buy a gun, or you may just end up in prison. Be wise and sensible.

Besides the Bible, the most important document ever written is the Constitution of the United States of America, because it is written as "Bible Application for Citizenship." Challenge that liberal media!
Christians STAND!

And, take up . . .

The challenge of dying to self and knowing when to stand.

Chapter 5

The Family Fussing

What Family?

What is a Family?

What is the fuss regarding the family?

Each of the three questions can cause a fuss! How many families might a person belong to? That certainly can create a conversation pregnant with contention, anger, and hostility.

As I originally began writing this chapter the Supreme Court of the United States was preparing to "define" or "redefine" family. There is a big fuss going on in the nation regarding marriage. Since the decision by our Supreme Court has now been made it will shape the "family" in America. Their decision is unBiblical. It will not change what God says about the family and marriage. It will not solve the mushrooming crisis over the family, or the many crises the families face daily. The relationship of love, partnership, sexual fidelity and other commitments between a man (a naturally born man) and woman (a naturally born woman) will not be strengthened. Families will be weakened and in some subcultures of the United States the FAMILY will be destroyed. Our nation is fussing over major issues regarding the family.

Since the original volume, we have seen a huge battle taking place over "gender identification" and how that plays out in our nation through ethics and morality or the lack thereof. For instance, we are now seeing questionable activity going on in public restrooms, and sports activities. Men pretending to be women! What kind of mindset is that? I'll tell you. It is the same as Sodom and Gomorrah of Biblical days. And, the judgment will be the same.

Here is a bit of wisdom for parents to teach their children:

If a child looks down to their feet and notices something between their legs that looks like a "worm" then the child needs to say, "I am a boy!" If the child looks down to their feet and notices something between their legs that looks like a "valley" then the child needs to say, "I am a girl!"

God made two genders – that's all. He, God the Creator, made humankind either MALE or FEMALE. That's it. That's the choices. All other choices are either Sick or Diabolical. Which are you? Which do you want your children to be? Normal, Sick or Diabolical?

While there is a fuss in our nation about "family" it still remains that an individual family will fuss. Families fuss over a quantum list of things – position, inheritance, control, methods, games to play; finances, discipline, kids, parents, schools, cars, sports, clothes, pets, vacations, work, houses, tooth paste, cookies, TV.

It begins when the honeymoon is over. When two people, in love and committed to live life together, as man and wife, settle in to their new home, reality sets in. Some differences are realized before the wedding but they become pronounced after the honeymoon. Day to day living reveals idiosyncrasies that bother one or the other, or both. Beliefs and attitudes emerge, which drive the behavior of the newlyweds.

After our honeymoon, Patricia and I returned to our small rental house in Florida. We needed groceries. So, we went to the Air Force BX on base and loaded our car trunk with groceries and household supplies. But the event was our first fuss as newlyweds. Coming from two different backgrounds, we had our own idea of what should go in the pantry. I wanted to splurge (which we could ill afford) and she wanted to conserve. We discovered our differences quickly. Those differences never diminished our love for each other.

If a couple learns to fight (or constructively dialog) fairly and resolve issues well, early on in the relationship, then they become empowered throughout their marriage. The solutions can be taught to the children in the home. But, on the other hand, if conflict is not handled well and fussing becomes the norm for the couple, it will also be the norm for the whole family until a crisis changes one or more in the family. The change is not always positive. The family could become severely broken or even involved in criminal action.

Offenses can accumulate if family members do not learn to resolve conflict through forgiveness. (See the last chapter of this book for Biblical steps toward reconciliation) The family can be beaten down, beaten up and torn apart in every way if fussing is not managed and even stopped.

Business associates must learn to give and take when possible. They need to learn communication skills, local mores, (standards) business policies, values, scruples, traditions, protocol, kindness, understanding, patience, even how to love (brotherly love) that co-worker so as to make forgiveness possible.

The Bible is clear about how we are to relate to each other, especially as family. Moses reminded the Israelites: *"You shall not take vengeance, nor bear any grudge against the children of your people, but you shall love your neighbor as yourself: I AM the LORD."* **(Leviticus 19:18 NKJV)** That is true for the Bible believing families in the twenty-first century as well. John, the Apostle reminds us that, *"If someone says, 'I love God,' and hates his brother, he is a liar; for he who does not love his brother whom he has seen, how can he love God whom he has not seen?"* **(1 John 4:20 NKJV)**

My family fussed as we were growing up. Mother and Daddy fussed. They fussed over money (or rather the lack of it) and whether or not mother would go back to work at Blue Bell Manufacturing making overalls. She couldn't drive and that would present a grave problem for her. My brothers fussed over cars, tools, and lawnmowers. My sisters fussed over washing dishes, cleaning yards and ironing. Daddy fussed with the alcoholic next door. Daddy fussed with some business owners from time to time. I was told there was a big fuss at a church they attended, but not his making. Now, isn't that ironic, my Daddy fussed with others? But there was no one to say to him, (*bless his pea picking heart, as we say in the South!*) "Fuss, fuss fuss. That is all I hear!" There was fussing over who to marry. There was fussing over school. There was fussing by many in my hometown. I wish we could all have taken the advice of my precious granddaughter, Abby, a few years ago who, as a young child, advised us when a couple in the crowd was about to have a fuss: "Just get over it!"

Dr. James Dobson, Founder of "Focus on the Family," and now founder and president of Family Institute, noted in one of his radio programs a few years ago, that conflict ought to be backed up ONE day. He was telling the story of a mother who "fussed" every Sunday with her daughter (or was it the daughter fussing with her Mom?) about what to wear to church on Sunday. The solution was to back it up to Saturday and decide what to wear. Dr. Dobson's comment caught my attention as a young father. My take away was: If we can see a fuss coming regarding decisions we are about to make, or actions we are about to take, we ought to discuss the issues, then "back it up" a few hours or a day, or a week, so that we can avoid the pressures that inflame the fuss.

There is one person who can ensure you that your life is free of fussing – YOU! The Bible exhorts all of us to *"Do all things without complaining and disputing. . ."* **(Philippians 2:14 NKJV)** Today's culture challenges all Christian families to STOP fussing. The better choice is to encourage each other, build up each other (edify) and take care of each other. *"Therefore, laying aside all malice, all deceit, hypocrisy, envy, and all evil speaking. . ."* **(1 Peter 2:1 NKJV)** You can do that!

This is a huge principle for families to follow. It takes specific, decisive action – lay aside – or simply put – "Lay your Fussing weapons down." Or we might say, "Place your tools to destroy others back in the box!" You see, according to the Scripture just quoted, when the tools or weapons of malice, deceit, hypocrisy (which always include lying), envy and evil speaking are put away, what do you have left? Just truth, bare naked truth that will set you free! One would have to be sick to not want to exchange war for peace, contention for tranquility.

Family fussing is part of the growth process for children. They learn to socialize, to work out differences early in life so that they can function at a higher level as they mature. Parents who give their children good skills in solving differences between themselves and other children will see great rewards when those children are in high school and beyond. The friction in childish fussing does allow parent and child, teacher and child, to bond in a way that develops the child's skills to discern, decide and devote.

Families which allow arguments to simply "work themselves out" or to be pushed down deeper, or "just sucked up and move on" will find young adults with pent up anger and hostility. Problems with job security, the rotting away of marriage bliss, and even actions of criminal proportion ensue from hostilities rooted in childhood experiences. Those childhood disputes, left unresolved, will come back to bite the personality who is now a young adult.

Some folks just push down inside their soul the anger and hurt of an episode that was never resolved. It might be being bullied in school. It might be a father or mother who abandoned the family. It might be a moral failure never confessed or a perpetration upon one's character, psyche, or physical body. Later, when a family crisis happens and the one injured is grieving or feeling despondent, fussing can erupt. It might be over furniture, or money, or land. The hurt and pain causes the victim of injury to respond to the fuss in a way that is less than mature. If he realizes how childish the fuss is and how subtle the work of spiritual darkness really is, then he can deal with the situation in a way to prevent future fussing. The Bible teaches us in Peter's first epistle, that as Christians we ought to:

> ". . . be of one mind, having compassion for one another; love as brothers, be tenderhearted, be courteous; not returning evil for evil or reviling for reviling, but on the contrary blessing, knowing that you were called to this, that you may inherit a blessing. For

> *He who would love life*
> *And see good days.*
> *Let him refrain his tongue from evil.*

And his lips from speaking deceit.
Let him turn away from evil and do good;
Let him seek peace and pursue it.
For the eyes of the Lord are on the righteous, And His ears are open to their prayers;
But the face of the Lord is against those who do evil." **(1 Peter 3:8-12 NKJV)**

Simply put, for us to do what Peter admonishes us to NOT do, is an act of futility (dealt with in chapter one). There are Biblical ways of dealing with the fuss. We need to be aware of how seriously God takes fussing among His family known as the church. Hear the Wisdom of God:

> **These six *things* the LORD hates, Yes, seven *are* an abomination to Him:**
> **A proud look, A lying tongue, Hands that shed innocent blood,**
> **A heart that devises wicked plans, Feet that are swift in running to evil,**
> **A false witness *who* speaks lies, And one who sows discord among brethren.**
> **Proverbs 6:16-19 (NKJV)**

See, God HATES discord among the family. We need to take this word as seriously as God was in giving it to us. We need to work at removing these things from our lives with the same fervor as wanting to avoid hell. If we do, we will be on our way to overcoming the fuss that brings discord.

84

Hear, again the WISDOM OF GOD, which is so much better than the wisdom of man. He says through the Apostle Paul, writing to a "struggling, troubled church:

> **"Dare any of you, having a matter against another, go to law before the unrighteous, and not before the saints? Do you not know that the saints will judge the world? And if the world will be judged by you, are you unworthy to judge the smallest matters? Do you not know that we shall judge angels? How much more, things that pertain to this life? If then you have judgments concerning things pertaining to this life, do you appoint those who are least esteemed by the church to judge? I say this to your shame. Is it so, that there is not a wise man among you, not even one, who will be able to judge between his brethren? But brother goes to law against brother, and that before unbelievers! Now therefore, it is already an utter failure for you that you go to law against one another. Why do you not rather accept wrong? Why do you not rather *let yourselves* be cheated?"**
> **1 Corinthians 6:1-7 (NKJV)**

On the surface we might react: "I don't want to be cheated, or wronged, no matter who it is!" And, in the flesh that is rightly stated. However, if we can see this picture through the eyes of love and faith and hope, then we can deny ourselves a victory; deliberately skirt the "dodge the bullet" moment and minister in the name of Christ to the one who gives the offense, the wrong, the cheat. Sometimes we have

85

to wade through the filthy swamp of a pagan world in order to minister to them. Do I do it perfectly? Of course not! Are there some who can? Absolutely! And, while most Christians in the United States will not have to wade very deep into the abyss of sinfulness, all of us will experience the moments we are called upon by the Spirit of God to DIE TO SELF and magnify HIS name for HIS glory.

THE HOME ought to be an example of those who accept . . .

The challenge of dying to self and knowing when to stand.

Chapter 6

Dying for and Standing for the Family

The basic fabric of any society is the family.

Let me say that again:

The basic fabric of any society is the family.

FAMILIES ARE WORTH DYING FOR!

Is one family valued over another? No, all FAMILIES are worth the cost we must pay because "Family" is God's idea. God desires to work through a family as well as individuals. However, we must understand that God's idea of family is ONE man and ONE woman and the children they bear and/or adopt. The term describing this family is "nuclear."[20] Merriam-Webster dictionary says: "a family group that consists only of father, mother, and children." Of course, I have used this term many times in sermons. When I looked it up to give a "vetted reference" the web site asked me, "What made you want to look up nuclear family? Please tell us where you read or heard it (including the quote, if possible.")[21]

That really caught my attention! It is impossible to detect emotions, tones and attitudes via electronic media, regardless of those "emoticons." This leads me to say there may be no hidden agenda with the dictionary folks. But, it sounds like something a parent would say to their school age child if they came home and used a "dirty word." Our culture is bleeding through into every aspect of our lives.

God desires for families to shape the neighborhood not for neighborhoods to raise a person's child. Paul the Apostle gives us the severity of a father [and single parents are not

---

[20] http://www.merriam-webster.com/dictionary/nuclear%20family

[21] Ibid.

off the hook here either] providing and protecting his family:

"But if anyone does not provide for his own, and especially for those of his household, he has denied the faith and is worse than an unbeliever." (1 Timothy 5:8)

FAMILIES FACE ISSUES THAT INFLUENCE AND AFFECT EACH MEMBER OF THE FAMILY!

God's idea of "Family" must be protected if our nation is to survive. This can be done in many ways. **First,** Christians need to pray for those who are shaping the family. We ought to pray for strong spiritual families. We must pray for the family to be equipped to face the cultural war we are in. **Families are facing financial ruin.** An ever-increasing mindset of "spending more than we make" stemming from a cultural lie that we can have everything "right now" and, a liberal government in control, are placing parents and children in a slave scenario**. Families must learn to overcome self-gratification** and replace it with sacrificial love. In a third wave of attack, our families are facing devastating emotional sabotage. Home and school, home and the workplace, home and church are no longer in sync with each other. The value systems are warped and do not fit. A **fourth** attack upon the family, which I have already alluded to, is the world of politics. In all three branches of government, we are faced with enemy profiles that are undermining the family. These enemies take the form of "socialism," "neo-facism," "communism," "unbridled consumerism," and "me-ism."

Political gain, and power, and prestige is the motivation for many of our servant leaders (it should NOT be but seems to be the job description for our politicians today) to cast away the family and family values for their own selfish goals.

In a **fifth realm of looking at the family** we see very few members of the family who know how to survive and care for themselves. Why is there so much unemployment? Why Who told the young adult to stay home and mooch off of their parents into their late twenties and thirties? Why are so many, including even boomers staying home and not working today? Oh, it's the pandemic. HOG WASH! We need to tell the government to get out of our business and protect us like the constitution demands. Government needs to get out of family control and control the borders and national defense. Read the constitution.

Who of the millions of millennials know how to survive if the government crashes? How will they feed themselves when the money runs out? How do you clean a chicken or a turkey in order to put it on the dinner table? Or, if it comes to it, how do you hunt and kill the rabbit that is left in your small wooded area – which may be your last meal? Families need time together for Dad and Mom to be able to teach the basic principles of life. Oh, that is, if the parents know what they are! I don't mean to be cynical. But do kids know how to care for the house? The family car? (I refuse to buy a car owned by a young family! – because most of them are trashed!)

Today, we need to find ways to encourage the family, equip the family and envelop the family with love – love for God, for themselves and the neighbors next door.

FAMILIES NEED AN ADVOCATE!
One of the battlegrounds for the family today is in the courtroom of every judge. Judges raise their hand (usually on a Bible) to "swear" or "affirm" that they will uphold the constitution of the United States. That means they uphold the laws of the land enacted by the Congress of the land who are placed in the office by the people of the land. They are

NOT there to legislate from the bench. Their department is the judicial branch of government NOT the legislative branch. Proverbs 16, written by King Solomon, teaches us several principles about our tongue which can be applied to the judges who serve us. Families need the advocacy of judges to keep the fabric of America strong. <u>Here are some of those principles:</u>

1. Hearts (not political agendas) ought to be prepared before we speak.
2. Our ways ought to be weighed in God's balances before we practice them.
3. Our thoughts ought to be established to keep us from following the flow of the culture.
4. Without humility we set ourselves up to fail.
5. It is better to fear the Lord than to fear man in order to have strength to depart from evil.
6. Wisdom is found in being pleasing to God, not man.
7. Justice has a far better payday than any amount we can get through bribery.
8. Rulers (includes judges) over us make God sick when they commit wickedness.
9. People will follow those who lead in righteousness.
10. Wisdom with understanding is far better than any kind of earthly money.
11. Those who serve with a haughty spirit will end in failure.
12. Our lips should speak the words that lead others to truth.

13. Our words can bring health to our nation.
14. If we follow only that which seems right in the eyes of man we create a culture of death.
15. We should always strive to not dig up evil, not sow strife, not bear false witness, not follow violence, and not be deceitful.
16. Aging should bring glory to a nation and senior living can do so when Christians follow the ways of righteousness.
17. Everyone can become better by being slow to get angry and using self-control.

Another advocate for the family is parents. A Dad and a Mom (one each male and one each female, NOT two dads and two moms – or three or four) is God's ideal. Family needs a healthy male role and a healthy female role leading the family in growth and maturity. Anything less is <u>a hotbed for confusion, conflict, dysfunction and destruction of the fibers that are used to build true community and a powerful nation.</u>

Today, the High School and University classroom is a brainwashing canteen. Some serve huge helpings of Critical Race Theory, teaching our kids to hate themselves. The majority of our parents today do not even know what CRT is and many of them do not care.

Pastors are yet another group of spokespersons for the family. Families are strengthened when pastors understand the true design of family as presented in the Bible. Good, expository preaching, and classes that are designed to teach people the role, structure, purpose and value of family will produce strong individuals who know how to lead businesses, the education system, political systems and the economy. We are NOT called to be WOKE pastors or people of God. WOKE is evil, teaching hatred. It is high time for pastors to rediscover their backbone and couple that with love in their hearts and preach the TRUTH!

FAMILIES SET THE STANDARDS FOR THE NATION.

Here is a great lesson from Nehemiah who was an effective leader and builder in the nation of Israel. The nation had been in political slavery, in Babylon and Persia for centuries. Now, God was about to do a new thing with the nation and with the FAMILIES. Nehemiah, along with Ezra and key leaders/fathers of the nation followed God through obedience to His Word to set the standards for the whole nation. They had "a mind to work" (4:6), hearts tuned in to God through prayer (4:9), a spirit of cooperation (4:6), a watchful eye (4:9), and a leader who was resolute to defeat the enemies of God. Nehemiah said:

> ". . . I positioned men behind the lower parts of the wall, at the openings; and I set the people according to their families, with their swords, their spears, and their bows. And I looked, and arose and said to the nobles, to the leaders and to the rest of the people "do not be afraid of them. Remember the Lord, great and awesome, and fight for your brethren your sons, your daughters, your wives, and your houses." (Nehemiah 4:13-14)

Regarding the family, he teaches us that we ought not to stoop to the level of those who are trying to destroy the family. We need to stand in face of all enemies and keep doing the great work of God through the family.

> "Now it happened when Sanballat, Tobiah, and Geshem the Arab, and the rest of our enemies heard that I had rebuilt the wall, and *that* there were no breaks left in it (though at that time I had not hung the doors in the gates), that Sanballat and Geshem sent to me saying, "Come, let us meet together among the villages in the plain of Ono." But they thought to do me harm. So I sent messengers to them, saying, "I am doing a great work, so that I cannot come down, why should the work cease while I leave it and go down to you?" But they sent me this message four times, and I answered them in the same manner." (Nehemiah 6:1-4)

Nehemiah – the rebuilder, Solomon - the King and the Apostle Paul give us insights on how we can take a stand for the family. We are bombarded every day. We need to practice putting on the whole armor of God and not only stand but to counter the culture. Nature teaches us how we are to protect our "family" as it does so. Birds, bees, cows and kangaroos, dogs and cats, even the ugly opossum and the beautiful eagle share with us their secrets in protecting their family. LEARN FROM GOD-CREATED NATURE HOW TO PROTECT YOUR FAMILY.

FAMILIES NEED TO LEARN HOW TO STAND!

If you mess with a bird, it is going to flee for protection.

Mess with a bee and you are going to get stung!

Mess with a dog or cat – you're gonna get bit or scratched.

Mess with a cow – you're gonna get horned or kicked.

Mess with a kangaroo – you're gonna get boxed.

Mess with a Christian leader – you're gonna get spiritually "whooped."

So, what do you do to protect you and your family from those "messing" with your values, your beliefs, your values? We have protection built in and provided for us.

"Therefore take up the whole armor of God, that you may be able to withstand in the evil day, and having done all to stand." (Ephesians 6:13)

Humility is the orientation to the grace of God. It helps to see the truth of the scripture found in James 4: 6 says,

> **"But He gives more grace. Therefore He says;**
> ***God resists the proud,***
> ***But gives grace to the humble."***

Just as a Rubik's Cube ® must be "oriented" in order to solve it, so we must be oriented by humility to receive the grace of God. The more we orientate to humility, the more we receive of His grace.

FAMILIES NEED TO LEARN HOW TO STAND! And, accept

The challenge of dying to self and knowing when to stand.

Fuss! Fuss! Fuss!

Chapter 7

The Faithful Fussing

The Holy Spirit (Third Person of the Trinity) shows us the reality of the fallen world we live in. He shows us (the Spirit of God is not an "it") right from wrong. He guides us toward the good and away from the evil way of life. He is the One who convinces us that we are sinners in the first place and then makes a way for us to hear the Gospel and experience the powerful saving redemption of Jesus the Son.

> **"It is always, and everywhere, wrong to target and kill the innocent . . . to be cruel and hateful, to enslave and oppress. It is always, and everywhere, right to be kind and just, to protect the lives of others, and to lay down your life for a friend."**

So said President George W. Bush, whom I respect for his stand against evil perpetrated upon our nation in 2001, early on in his presidency, by militant and evil Muslims who hate the United States of America.[22]

In the next few pages, I will describe two groups of people – Believers in Christ, and non-believers. As I write about these two groups of people who make up our world, it is of utmost importance to know that most of the fussing in the future will be between these two classes – a worldwide cultural characteristic, who are totally opposite in beliefs, ideologies, philosophies, morals, ethics, and activities. Why is that so? Glad you asked!

The climax of civilization is imminent. The "end of times" will come based on the reality of Jesus Christ as the ONE and ONLY Savior of the world; the true King of kings, and LORD of lords, the Incarnate (infleshment – yes, God came down and dwelt among us, became one of us – hence Christmas) God, who spoke the world into existence (evolution is a LIE), and will consummate the world with His wrath and judgment.

---

[22] David Aikman, *Man of* Faith, W. Publishing Group, Division of Thomas Nelson, Inc.; Nashville: 2004, p. 155.

This chapter has two parts: TRUE FAITH and FALSE FAITH. People can be faithful to anything. So, we need to distinguish between truth and error. The dynamics of fussing are the same in both camps. However, the ramifications of that fuss are vastly different both now and in eternity.

Who are the Faithful? Now, that is a big fuss in itself! When I talk about "the Faithful" in this book, I'm alluding to faith in terms of a person's religious experience and relationships. The idea of a "faith community" can be healthy in the sense that it consists of people in the Christian Faith. These include Baptists, Methodists, Presbyterians, Episcopalians, Assemblies, some other denomination, or even independent faith groups. Sometimes, these believers in Christ come together to accomplish such projects as relieving the hurt and pain of a hurricane-torn Gulf Coast by a Katrina. Or, it could be meeting the needs created by a sixty-seven-tornado-torn Alabama, or a hurricane-torn New England by a Sandy, or a two-mile wide tornado destroying Moore, Oklahoma, or an eighty-mile stretch of tornadoes in Alabama, or a tsunami in Japan.

Let's look at:

A. TRUE FAITH

While this chapter addresses both true faith and false faith, I want to focus heavily on the faith of the Christian community, which is, as I purport in this book, the TRUE FAITH. I do so because Christian faith is faith in the one true God, the God of Abraham, Isaac, and Jacob. It is the faith in Jesus Christ who is God in the flesh; who was born of a Virgin, God in the flesh, who lived a perfect life to produce true righteousness; God in the flesh, who died a sacrificial death on the Cross, who rose from the dead of His own volition, and ascended back to Heaven, and who will return to Earth someday as the rightful owner and King over the whole world. And, without being fussy, I challenge anyone to prove to me and the world that there is any other god who is alive and created the universe!

Jesus said to him, "I am the way, the truth, and the life. No one comes to the Father except through me. (John 14:6 NKJV)

I do so because we Christians need to position ourselves to be true witnesses. We need to stand in order to have the reputation which reflects the Love of God. True love does not tolerate sin that destroys an individual, a family, or a nation. God's love changes the world for the better then the BEST. Therefore, we must STAND!

It is a given, then that we have to know what we are standing for. Sin brings death. Sin is anything we do against Holy God. We all need forgiveness. I speak of that in Chapter Thirteen. And, as we engage in fussing, it is most likely that we will sin, not only against God, but against a fellow human being. Therefore, we need to seek and ask for forgiveness. The Bible says:

> **"And whenever you stand praying, if you have anything against anyone, forgive him, that your Father in heaven may also forgive you your trespasses. But if you do not forgive, neither will your Father in heaven forgive your trespasses"** **(Mark 11:25-26 NKJV).**

Church signs invite the community in various ways. One says, "Come Worship with Us!" Another reads: "Come Fellowship with Us!" Still another says, "Find Life Here!" Never,

Fussing can destroy a church.

have I seen a sign that says, "Come FUSS with us!" And, yet, that is what people eventually find in a church. Churches don't mean to fuss, usually, they just do. They experience differences of opinion, wrong decisions, bad choices and a fuss erupts. Fussing can destroy a church. A church engaged in fussing can guarantee that their community will be less likely to become Christian.

Down through the centuries there has been fussing among the faithful. After three revivals had concluded, in a small town, the three pastors of the Methodist, Baptist and Presbyterian churches, were discussing the results with one another. The Methodist minister said, "The revival worked out great for us! We gained four new families." The Baptist preacher said, "We did better than that! We gained six new families." The Presbyterian pastor said, "Well, we did even better than that! We got rid of our ten biggest trouble makers.

Let me add that within each denomination and in the local independent families of faith are many issues that cause division and conflict. Some of the infighting is simply the Faithful, who know Biblical truth, taking a STAND for that truth. Here are some of the foundations of the TRUE FAITH:

1. The privilege to DEFEND the FAITH (and here, again, I'm talking about the Christian Faith – the one and only true faith) is paramount in building a Free nation. In the United

States of America religious freedom allows anyone to express their religious beliefs without fear of reprisal, unless some crime is committed in the exercise of that religion. An example within the Christian context would be how one reacts to a social issue such as abortion. It is never right to kill someone who practices the evil of abortion to prove that you are making a "stand against this crime on humanity."

In the False Faith camp an example would be "mercy killing" by Islamic leaders. Another would include murderous activity, or the slaying of animals in a cultic fashion. Life is held in high esteem in the United States of America. However, this writer must confess his total disgust and shame over how our nation of the brave and free, in the last two decades, has allowed the erosion of this principle. Such erosion is aberrant to a capitalistic society.

> **1 Corinthians 1:10 (NKJV)**
>
> [10] Now I plead with you, brethren, by the name of our Lord Jesus Christ, that you all speak the same thing, and *that* there be no divisions among you, but *that* you be perfectly joined together in the same mind and in the same judgment.

2. The election of FAITHFUL Christians to serve in the various political offices of the land, from city to national service, is essential to sustaining freedom. Why? Because it is the Judeo-Christian mindset that this nation was founded on and is the only mindset that will preserve the nation as our founding fathers designed it. This writer believes that the United States is as someone rightly refers to Israel and Britain and the United States as "client nations." A client nation is one God chooses to accomplish His will and purposes during a given period of time.

I met Tony Perkins in Birmingham, Alabama recently. I was impressed with his speech. He portrayed himself as a man who loves the United States of America and his "fellow man." Therefore, I read his book, *Personal Faith, Public Policy*, co-authored with Harry R. Jackson, Jr.[23] We share many of the same convictions. He, of course has the public service in government to validate his writings. Tony says, "Christians are called to perform a "prophetic" role in modern-day culture." He explains that in the Bible we see prophets as God's spoke persons. Much like the prophets,

---

[23] Tony Perkins & Harry R. Jackson, Jr., *Personal Faith, Public Policy*, Frontline, 2008, pp 43-44.

"the church is the custodian of the national conscience."[24] I agree with Perkins that Christians are "to act and believe as though each one of us has a prophetic assignment to the nation that begins right where we live and work."[25]

Our forefathers founded this nation and wrote the Constitution based on Judeo-Christian beliefs. Let me give you one example: The United States has three branches of government which are based on Isaiah 33:22, **"(For the Lord is our Judge, The Lord is our Lawgiver, The Lord is our King; He will save us):"** Now, do you see why it is important that we know and understand the Bible? Does it not make good sense to defend this treasure that has been handed to us? The **Judicial, the Legislative, and the Executive branches of government** must remain the basis for governing ourselves as a "free people," or we fall to the hands of a socialistic elite group of leaders, or a tyrannical dictator. And, may I add, all three branches have "servants" who swore to defend the Constitution of the United States of America. It is NOT, let me repeat, "NOT" the Constitution that defends the office; nor the dignity of its citizens; the

---

[24] Quote from Paul Harvey, heard and remembered by the author as he listened to "Paul Harvey News!"
[25] Ibid, Perkins

office defends the constitution. If a politician does not understand that and if immigrants do not understand that, they need training in United States values and laws. PERIOD! The President is under the constitution no matter what Harvard teaches! The Senators are UNDER the constitution no matter which man or woman is elected. The Judge is under the constitution no matter the level of his/her judiciary service. To reverse that is unethical and criminal! Period!

3. The FAMILY must be kept as the primary unit of the nation. To do otherwise will guarantee destruction. God can and will work in any governmental body on the earth. He does not approve of every activity or policy within a human government, but ALLOWS men and women to rise to power to accomplish HIS purposes. God demonstrated His will and purpose for government in Israel's early years. Yet Israel decided to be "like all the other nations" and desired a king (human king). Israel and the divided kingdom of Judah both had good kings and bad kings. We can see that as the nation of Israel honored God the nation was blessed. So, it was with other nations. People had higher quality of life when "good kings" ruled. Homes were strong.

Then, too, we can see as we read history, that when nations turned their back on God they were destroyed or simply slid off the scene of history. Look at the world powers: Chaldeans, Egyptians, Assyrians, Babylonians, Persians, Greece, Rome, England, Germany, Japan, and the United States of America. All of these refused to honor and recognize God's authority over them, or came to that point at the close of their national life. They simply refused to honor Him by embracing principles found through His revelation to prophets, preachers and ultimately through His Son, Jesus Christ and recorded in His Holy Word. Judgment fell or is falling upon those nations.

God has always watched the nations. He knows what they do and don't do. He allows the leaders of nations to be righteous or unrighteous and see the fruit of their labors. He allows men and women to come to power. It is not always His perfect will for a certain person to be in power. Men make decisions and God lets them have their way. He gives us all air to breathe. We choose where and when to breathe, unless, of course, we are forced by some other human or some human circumstance to do otherwise. He destroys nations and national leaders when He chooses, because He is sovereign.

Paul, the Apostle was preaching at Mars Hill, according to the Scriptures, attempting to make the "UNKNOWN GOD" known to his hearers. (Exactly what I am doing in this book!) Luke recorded it this way:

"Then Paul stood in the midst of the Areopagus and said, "Men of Athens, I perceive that in all things you are very religious;
for as I was passing through and considering the objects of your worship, I even found an altar with this inscription: **TO THE UNKNOWN GOD.**
Therefore, the One whom you worship without knowing, Him I proclaim to you:
God, who made the world and everything in it, since He is Lord of heaven and earth, does not dwell in temples made with hands.
Nor is He worshiped with men's hands, as though He needed anything, since He gives to all life, breath, and all things.
And He has made from one blood every nation of men to dwell on all the face of the earth, and has determined their preappointed times and the boundaries of their dwellings,
so that they should seek the Lord, in the hope that they might grope for Him and find Him, though He is not far from each one of us;
for in Him we live and move and have our being, as also some of your own poets have said, 'For we are also His offspring.' (Acts 17:22-28a NKJV).

The prophets declared: *"The Lord is slow to anger;"* (**Nahum 1:3 NKJV**) and *"Who can stand before His indignation?"* (**Nahum 1:6 NKJV**)   God is always patient. He waits for leaders to come to Him, to repent of sin, and lead their nation to repent of sin.   When they continually refuse, then He brings judgment upon them.

4. The RIGHT to LIFE and the right for each individual to PROTECT themselves from injustice. Abortion is a fuss mostly with other denominations within the Christian ranks, such as Methodists who embrace abortion, governmental bodies, especially the United States Congress, and Supreme Court and the unbelieving world at large, who all reject what the Bible says about Life.   Since 1973, and the deadly ruling of the United States Supreme Court in <u>Roe</u> v. <u>Wade,</u> legalizing abortion all the way through to the last month of pregnancy, over 60 million babies have been killed in their mother's womb.   Southern Baptists have taken a strong stand against this death decision.   Resolutions have been adopted by the SBC that removed any question about their belief that taking a life before it is born is murder.[26]

---

[26] Resolutions are simply that. The Southern Baptist Convention drafts a resolution, the messengers approve or disapprove the resolution and the churches use the resolution as a means to shape their action in the local setting. Since Roe v. Wade, 1973 there

The SBC has been on the cutting edge of being involved in alternatives to abortion. Because of the structure of the convention, most of the involvement would have to be documented by each local church in every community throughout the states. Such practices as: adoption; health care centers for unwed mothers; support of *Sav-a-Life;*[27] and other Christian organizations tangibly answer the questions about the sanctity of human life.

5. Capital Punishment is a fuss that has lesser intensity at the present time but is an issue among SBC members. Most of the SBC would support Capital Punishment as a deterrent to crime.

6. Gambling is a sin and causes great sinful actions including fussing. Let me share a personal example of the Faithful fussing. A couple of years ago, I was in a fuss

---

have been many such resolutions adopted in opposition to the Supreme Court decision. An example is found in the 2003 SBC Annual (June 17-18, 2003) meeting in Phoenix, AZ., on page 74-75.

[27] Sav-a-Life is the ™ for the organization that promotes "a comprehensive pregnancy care ministry that is dedicated to offering free and confidential services in a loving environment to women, men, and families facing an unplanned pregnancy. The website is: http://savalife.org/ .

between the gambling crowd and the faithful—more like a fight. The fuss was between Alabamians who opposed gambling and some outside influencers with BIG money, who wanted gambling legalized in the state. Those of us who are adamantly opposed to gambling of any kind were invited to a rally in Montgomery, on Tuesday, February 23, 2010. We came together for the rally on the steps of the state capitol in Montgomery. It was to be about an hour. The crowd was to show the legislators that there is strength in the opposition to gambling. The then Governor, Bob Riley was to speak. He is very much opposed to gambling and was taking a strong stand against it. I arrived on time with a friend. The Pro-gambling crowd had arrived even earlier and had taken all the front area, the steps, and platform. They were shouting many derogatory things, holding signs in an attempt to intimidate and misinform those in opposition to gambling. The "Pro Gambling crowd" displayed a lot of anger.

The question is raised, "Who paid these people to show up?" Much contention was felt, heard, and seen. Someone was trying to get the people to move back (off the platform – the porch to the capitol) so the governor could get out to speak. No one budged. I decided to make my way to the porch and see better what was going on. The attitudes were those of spoiled brats or school ground fussing between brats and bullies and their victims. As I positioned myself on the porch, next to what seemed to be the loudest man there, I decided to engage him in conversation. I commented that the Gambling issue is NOT about jobs as they were claiming. He retorted – "Do you have a job? Where do you work?" I fumbled for the words, "I'm self-employed," because I didn't see the value of telling him I was a Baptist preacher and missionary.

He was joined by a woman and the two of them launched a verbal attack against me. I could not get them to reason with me. He assumed and said, "Where do you go to church?" I told him and he replied, "I'm going to be there Sunday. Is that okay with you?" I said, "Sure, come on!" to which he sneered. He made it a "race" issue rather than a gambling issue. I wanted to change the subject, because I knew he was playing the race card on my faith. I asked him where he worked. He replied that he was on welfare and that my taxes were paying him. Of course, I sensed he was being facetious.

And since that time the gambling crowd in Alabama, has tried to say, "Let the people have a voice!" meaning let it come to a vote at the ballot box. We did and we spoke as a state against gambling. But they come back every year and try to get gambling legalized in Alabama. Now, they may win since they know how to "stuff" the ballot boxes as evidenced by the elections of 2020.

In it all, I saw the fuss was futile and that I was not making any progress. I realized later that at least I had quieted him by getting him into a "one on one dialog." Since I had no personal relationship with him, I backed away saying, "This is a useless conversation!" As I see it, something WAS accomplished that day. The rally only intensified the fuss and possibly made each side dig in their heels to win the battle over gambling. Conservatives were challenged to win the battle and we did! I learned that to resolve these issues, true Biblical principles of dealing with conflict would have to be employed.

7. Health Care has become a major issue and must be addressed by the Faithful. Obamacare, so called, was one of the worst demands ever introduced to the American scene. It is a political plague. It is an atrocity with built in freedom-

115

destroyers. At minimum, the fuss is about the United States Constitution, which primarily gives our "government" the power to protect our nation. It does not give the Congress the right to infringe upon the personal lives of the citizens of this free land. The fuss ranges from employers firing employees, to truckers threatening to stage a protest on the beltway in Washington, D.C. (This never materialized, but imagine if it had; Trucks move America!). Just think how ludicrous it sounds: "We have to pass it in order to see what's in it." That in of itself should have ended that fuss. The day it was signed into law, and people began to "get their insurance" the program was flawed. To this day, the computers that handle this monster do not serve our people well. How can a nation fall for such as this? Why was there not some folks STANDING against such evil? If business leaders and the working class of people had taken a stand we would not have such a mess to contend with. Sometimes we have to STAND!

Now, our health is wrapped around a pandemic called Covid 19, and Covid Omicron. The CDC (Center for Disease Control) is the voice "for the people based on science" and is one of the biggest shams in American medical history. Bigger than Obama Care. It is all about control and the national leaders along with the media organizations are purporting unnatural and "unscientific" actions upon our nation. Violation of the U.S. Constitution is paramount. **Doctors are duped.** People are void of common sense. We are coming out of the pandemic and the CDC is still trying to control America. Congress is in a fuss about it. Governors are fussing about it. Business people are fussing. School Boards are fussing with parents. Employers are fussing with Employees and the so-called President of the United States ("so-called" because he was not legally elected -the election was stolen) is issuing mandates regarding wearing masks and getting vaccinated. Unconstitutional! It is a page taken out of the Roman Empire's government control handbook. In that day, if a "worker" did not take a pinch of salt and offer it to the Caesar and say, "Caesar is Lord!," then that person did not have a job. Never did I think I'd see this in the USA in my lifetime. Never!

Fussing abounds from the HIGH Court to the dinner table in America. And the fuss will continue into the next administration and beyond.

8. Homosexuality is a despicable sin and leads to a painful and destructive fuss. As I write this book the issue of

117

homosexuality has grown in severity and in practice. Most people of the Christian faith do fuss, either with each other or between groups of different faith. Most Christian groups are fussing over the issue of homosexuality. At stake is what they do with the Bible which clearly forbids human beings from engaging in homosexual activity. One writer for the more liberal side of the Presbyterian family of faith states:

> The Presbyterian Church (USA) is generally more LGBT-welcoming than the more conservative Presbyterian Church in America, the denomination claimed by the "conscious choices" minister who (unlike his openly gay brother) rejects his attraction to men.[28]

On March 17, 2015 the Presbyterian Church (U.S.A.) voted to redefine marriage thus succumbing to the pressures of an unbiblical minority, following Episcopalians and Lutherans in previous years. Methodists are still barring such advocates from ministry roles. Southern Baptists, evangelical independent Baptists, and many National Baptist groups embrace the truth of the Bible and stand strong against the LGBT (now LGBTQ) political agenda.

---

[28]
http://www.advocate.com/politics/religion/2015/01/13/tennessee-vote-brings-presbyterian-church-usa-closer-agreement-marriage

No sooner than the announcement of the reversing of DOMA (Defense of Marriage Act, enacted in 1996) by The United States Supreme Court in 2013 came to the ears of the American people did the attorney general of California take a victory lap, laughing all the way through it. She is now the Vice President of the United States.

The only thing left intact by the high court is the right of states to deny acknowledgement of same-sex marriages. That did not stop hundreds of homosexuals from gathering at the steps of the capitols across the nation to celebrate their victory. The High Court's ruling in mid-2013 on this serious matter opened the gates for a multitude of crises in our culture. The Boy Scouts of America has made a devastating decision to allow gays (a good word that has been stolen by the Homosexual community) into their ranks. The once all boys organization which taught youngsters morality and Godly principles are just one more victim to the immoral agenda of the Left Wing of American politics. It will fail.

The Ethics and Religious Liberty Commission states:

On May 15, 2013, Dr. Richard Land, president of the Ethics & Religious Liberty Commission, sent a letter to

119

Wayne Brock, chief scout executive of the Boy Scouts of America, and Wayne Perry, president of the BSA, expressing "strident opposition" to a proposed resolution to eliminate the organization's ban on admitting for membership youth who are open or avowed homosexuals.[29]

The SBC followed that action with a strong resolution at the 2013 Convention in Houston, Texas.[30] Dr. Frank Page, Executive Director of the SBC Executive Committee clarifies the SBC position in an Article from SBCLIFE, online.[31]

The Supreme Court of the United States of America by their decision in 2015 regarding "same sex marriage" (which by the way is an anomaly = an incongruity; a glitch, an abnormality), placed our nation in the cross hairs of God's judgment. What were they thinking? The last report I have is the cities of Sodom and Gomorrah are still in a desolate, dust filled, ash heap in the Middle East.

---

[29] https://erlc.com/article/ltr-bsa-homosexuals-2013-05-15

[30] http://www.sbc.net/resolutions/613

[31] http://www.sbclife.net/Articles/2014/12/sla13

Fuss! Fuss! Fuss!

Those judges who voted to give "rights" to homosexuals are now restfully thinking, "We survived that one! No judgment upon us." My answer: "NOT so fast Mr. Supreme Court Justice. God's judgment is sometimes slow in coming, because He is a patient, loving God."

And, now we see homosexual activity creeping in at every level of our life. Even the once family friendly, conservative film makers Hallmark has succumbed and show homosexual couples in their movies. They too will see a downturn and downfall.

Gender issues are paramount. Men desiring to go into Women's restrooms is a sick proposition. We need men who will stand against any establishment that allows such wickedness and tell them that they will not do business with them if it is allowed and that if it happens while their wife or daughter is shopping in their store there will be repercussions. There are TWO genders – male and female. Only TWO. What a sicko we have in the cabinet of Joe Biden.

The issue is not **HATE!** We Christians don't hate people. We hate sin and what it does to destroy people. Hate crimes are wrong as is the practice of homosexuality. We must be aware today as we stand for The Faith that many will attempt to dissuade Christians from taking such a stand against homosexuality by saying such things as "Oh, we need to love everybody." Or "We need to never condemn anyone!" Or, "You shouldn't judge!" I can agree with these statements and do, if we take them as they are supposed to be understood in the Biblical context. We do love sinners. We can and should hate sin, no matter what sin it is. We should not condemn anyone. We should condemn, not condone the sin of people. We really don't have to: God says, "You are condemned already [because of sin]." One that I certainly can't agree to and it has been proven false is: "They are born that way!" as if there is a "gay gene." We all know John 3:16. We should know John 3:17. We should help people experience Romans 7 so that they can experience Romans 8:1, "there is therefore now, no condemnation to those who are Christ."

But, we should not overlook the rest of the Bible's teaching on homosexuality which includes:

> **"The sexually immoral, men who practice homosexuality, enslavers, liars, perjurers, and whatever else is contrary to sound doctrine," (1 Timothy 1:10 ESV)**

122

Therefore, God gave them up in the lusts of their hearts to impurity, to the dishonoring of their bodies among themselves, because they exchanged the truth about God for a lie and worshiped and served the creature rather than the Creator, who is blessed forever! Amen. For this reason God gave them up to dishonorable passions. For their women exchanged natural relations for those that are contrary to nature; and the men likewise gave up natural relations with women and were consumed with passion for one another, men committing shameless acts with men and receiving in themselves the due penalty for their error. (Romans 1:24-27 ESV)

You shall not lie with a male as with a woman; it is an abomination. (Leviticus 18:22 ESV)

The two angels came to Sodom in the evening, and Lot was sitting in the gate of Sodom. When Lot saw them, he rose to meet them and bowed himself with his face to the earth and said, "My lords, please turn aside to your servant's house and spend the night and wash your feet. Then you may rise up early and go on your way." They said, "No; we will spend the night in the town square." But he pressed them strongly; so they turned aside to him and entered his house. And he made them a feast and baked unleavened bread, and they ate. But before they lay down, the men of the city, the men of Sodom, both young and old, all the people to the last man, surrounded the house. And they called to Lot,

> **"Where are the men who came to you tonight? Bring them out to us, that we may know them." (Genesis 19:1-38 ESV)**
>
> **If a man lies with a male as with a woman, both of them have committed an abomination; they shall surely be put to death; their blood is upon them. (Leviticus 20:13 ESV)**

SBC churches that have been hosting Boy Scouts' meetings in their facilities will now ask the Boy Scouts to leave their facilities. Why? Because, the leadership of Boy Scouts caved to political correctness and the LGBT agenda. Let's suppose that a secular group wanted to use my office facility (whether it is a church or associational office or a private business meeting room). I or any one in charge of these rooms could give permission for this group to use the room to show training movies or the like. One day this group decides to show a movie that is not in keeping with the faith beliefs of the owner of the building. So, the owner (me or someone else) has the right and the integrity to ask the group to leave the building (not use the facility) and show their non-acceptable movie elsewhere. That is what churches are doing and rightly so!

These same churches will find other ways to minister to these boys and their leaders by such ministries as decades old Royal Ambassadors. This author agrees with these decisions. This author also predicts that Boy Scouts will decline in the next few years and may be defunct very soon.

Businesses have seen the power of the voice of people of FAITH when we speak out against homosexuality. Home Depot, Radio Shack, Ford Motor Company, all have seen the stand that the church can make. Some have responded positively to our stand and are still in business. Others have refused to change their policies (Radio Shack is now out of business) and are paying the price.

Issues, issues and more issues. That's life. But, the Godly and Holy life calls for us to take a stand for the faith, for the Word of God and for morality.

> **"But if anyone seems to be contentious, we have no such custom, nor *do* the churches of God. Now in giving these instructions I do not praise *you*, since you come together not for the better but for the worse. For first of all, when you come together as a church, I hear that there are divisions among you, and in part I believe it. For there must also be factions among you, that those who are approved may be recognized among you."**
> **(1 Corinthians 11:16-19 NKJV)**

> "For I fear lest, when I come, I shall not find you
> such as I wish, and *that* I shall be found by you
> such as you do not wish; lest *there be*
> contentions, jealousies, outbursts of wrath,
> selfish ambitions, backbitings, whisperings,
> conceits, tumults; lest, when I come again, my
> God will humble me among you, and I shall
> mourn for many who have sinned before and
> have not repented of the uncleanness,
> fornication, and lewdness which they have
> practiced."
> (2 Corinthians 12:20-21 NKJV)

So, we must deal with these powerful fusses going on in our nation. With any number of people, from the small family to the community where they live to the nation there are going to be fussing. It is inevitable that fussing and conflict of all sorts is bound to happen. But, we need to learn to resolve them.

Next we need to explore:

B. FALSE FAITH

The same idea of a "faith community" can be unhealthy when the people of a cult or false religion unite to destroy other kinds of faith in the world. What is a cult? It is any religious organization that does NOT accept Jesus Christ of Nazareth, as God in the flesh (Divine), crucified for sins of humanity, raised again the Third Day, sits with the Father in

126

Heaven and is coming again for His Church. What is a false religion? A false religion is any group of people who share religious beliefs other than Christianity. Because there is only ONE God and He is the Father, co-equal with the Son Jesus Christ and the Holy Spirit, these cannot be two "true Gods."   It includes such religions as Buddhism, Confucianism, Hinduism, New Age movement, Zen and the like. When the whole world is considered, the issue is "Which religion is right?"

Muslims fuss with everybody. Muslims are now in every country of the world. They are dominant in the Middle East and much of Africa. Whole nations such as Iran, Iraq, Turkey, Saudi Arabia, Pakistan, Afghanistan and many more are predominantly Muslim.

Christians make a fuss with other groups over who is Lord. Some religions don't fuss with anyone because their very nature is docile. They are pacifists.

It is pertinent at this point to make a distinction between "fussing" and "the defense of the faith."

God would have us to defend our reason for having hope in the Gospel and faith in Christ.

> *But sanctify the Lord God in your hearts, and*
> *always be ready to give a defense to everyone who*
> *asks you a reason for the hope that is in you, with*
> *meekness and fear;*
>
> *having a good conscience, that when they defame*
> *you as evildoers, those who revile your good*
> *conduct in Christ may be ashamed.*
> *For it is better, if it is the will of God, to suffer for*
> *doing good than for doing evil.*
> *(1 Peter 3:15-17 (NKJV)*

As Peter reminds us, we ought to do this with meekness, which is self-control, and fear, Godly reverence for our Father in Heaven whom we represent. When we defend our faith, it is not to be in a fussing or argumentative mode. Rather, it should be done, spiritually, logically, compassionately, intelligently, truthfully and boldly. Fussing over the Bible will never win a soul. Defending THE faith will always bear fruit or bring results. Either, we win the lost person to THE faith or, THE faith will be so offensive to the unbeliever, he will reject both the Gospel and the Witness, and/or retaliate.

The Standard, the litmus test IS:
"What do you do with Jesus?"

Fussing (not true defense of the faith or Christian Apologetics) about or "over" the Gospel and the Christian

Faith is futile and fails in its very nature. It ought to be avoided at all costs and at all times, with all people.

Focusing on the geographical area of a single country confines the fuss to limited venues for fussing. Some countries have zero tolerance (hence no religious freedom – and I always have to ask the leaders of those countries – "What are you afraid of – The Truth?") Nations without religious freedom are in themselves bound – bound to tyranny and a godless fundamentalism of human philosophy.

Some countries have very little tolerance of faith groups of any kind and rather discourage the people in pursuing religious things. We call these governments Fascism, Socialism or Communism. These countries fit the term fatalistic.

Fascism, a political view that believes the government should control everything is seen in a country like Germany under the leadership of Adolf Hitler. Communism, which teaches that people are best served by BIG government and owns everything, represented by Russia, Cuba, China, Venezuela and North Vietnam claim a huge part of the world's population. Communist leaders such as Marx,

Lenin, Stalin, Castro, all had as their goal world domination. Socialism is found in Europe and Canada. It dominates peoples' lives like Fascism and Communism. All three forms of government destroy the economy and infrastructure of a nation. When freedom is removed then fussing usually is diminished by the "sword" which leaves the people without hope. When land, buildings and factories are owned by the government there is little or no incentive to produce, or take care of or rebuild anything.

Then there is the nation which purports religious freedom and allows different faith groups to fuss with each other, the Great United States of America. Our country however is being attacked from within as well as without. Out of the White House and a liberal Congress, and a liberal Judicial Branch come unconstitutional and un-American decrees, orders, rulings and laws that destroy the freedom established by our constitution and protected until now by our political leaders. Our founding fathers built this country on a solid foundation, Biblical principles. Now those foundations are being destroyed. The Bible asks, "If the foundations are destroyed, what can the righteous do?" **(Psalm 11:3 NKJV)**

And, further the Bible guides us:

"O Timothy! Guard what was committed to your trust, avoiding the profane *and* idle babblings and contradictions of what is falsely called knowledge-- by professing it some have strayed concerning the faith. Grace *be* with you. Amen."
(1 Timothy 6:20-21 (NKJV)

"But avoid foolish and ignorant disputes, knowing that they generate strife.
And a servant of the Lord must not quarrel but be gentle to all, able to teach, patient,
in humility correcting those who are in opposition, if God perhaps will grant them repentance, so that they may know the truth, and *that* they may come to their senses *and escape* the snare of the devil, having been taken captive by him to *do* his will."
2 (Timothy 2:23-26 NKJV)

"Remind them to be subject to rulers and authorities, to obey, to be ready for every good work,
to speak evil of no one, to be peaceable, gentle, showing all humility to all men.

Our founding fathers built this country on a solid foundation, Biblical principles.

131

For we ourselves were also once foolish, disobedient, deceived, serving various lusts and pleasures, living in malice and envy, hateful and hating one another." (Titus 3:1-3 NKJV)

Families of FAITH must take up . . .

. . . The challenge of dying to self and knowing when to stand.

Chapter 8

Dying to Self and STANDING . . .

. . . to Be Faithful

Fussing and strife can and do "ruin" relationships. God wants us to remind each other to avoid fussing when possible. But, more profitably, we need to remind ourselves of this important truth in the heat of the moment. If we take the following admonition seriously it means that we really value our relationships. The Bible says:

"Remind *them* of these things, charging *them* before the Lord not to strive about words to no profit, to the ruin of the hearers."

2 Timothy 2:14 (NKJV)

One of the reasons we ought to die to self and be faithful to the Lord and to our earthly relationships is given as a proverb:

"A brother offended *is harder to win* than a strong city, And contentions *are* like the bars of a castle."

Proverbs 18:19 (NKJV)

Patricia and I have five precious grandchildren. Our daughter and her husband gave us two beautiful, smart, and energetic girls. Our son and his wife gave us triplets – two beautiful, smart and full of life girls and a very good looking, creative and in the minority boy. One day while our daughter's family was visiting and we were talking "books," the two oldest granddaughters asked me if they were going to be in my new book (this one)! I told them they were and they seemed to be glad. Recently their mother asked me if they were in the book. I said, "Well, your girls sure want to be included." To that she told me a story that had just happened. The girls were at home and decided to play outside. The oldest led the way. Her sister was trailing slowly. Since she was not going as fast as she thought her sister should be, and since she had been waiting some time holding the door for the younger, she let it go. In a minute, the young sibling was back in the house crying to her mom.

134

Mom asked her what was the matter, to which the offended younger exclaimed through tears, "She wouldn't bother to hold the door for me!" Mom wanted to know why and the younger responded, "She said she wouldn't hold the door for someone who would not come out as fast as they should." That prompted their mother to bring them together and ask, "Which of the Fruit of the Spirit did that little episode fit?" The girls replied, "None of them!"

I suppose, being the understanding grandparent that I am, they meant that they did not respond rightly to each other. I may be wrong. But I do believe their mom meant for them to note that the fruit of "patience" and "self-control" were not employed.

When we fuss and fight, we shut people out. Sometimes we might even shut them in as the story above reveals. Our contentious spirit and words build bars around us so that people cannot get in. Unless people get in, no love relationship is built.

Have you been on one of those "people movers" at the airport? I have. It is fun to ride and pass all the walking folks. I thought about that recently as I was on one of them:

> *Solutions can be found in the midst of fussing.*

How great it would be if we had some "thought movers" and "attitude movers" like that. A person could just hop on and get their thoughts moving faster toward the truth. Attitude could be changed in a moment which would rescue people for eternity. The reality is: <u>if we can get our attitudes and thoughts to quickly line up with Scripture, then see people as God created them, THAT becomes **"the attitude and thinking mover"** to rescue us from a futile fuss.</u> It is also a way to earn the right to share the Gospel with people in an effective way. If we earn that right, and then share the Gospel out of love, and in a way that God can use it, people will be delivered from their sin.

Solutions can be found in the midst of fussing. Usually, it takes time and energy to resolve conflict. Foolish debates usually have NO profit to either person involved in fussing. Note this from a very devoted apostle as he teaches about the futility of fussing and why we should die to self. The following summary, from the writers of the *Life Application Bible*, helps us to see what we Christians need to understand if we are going to make an impact on our culture:

Paul also referred to *genealogies* in his warning to Timothy. It might be that the false teachings in Crete, Ephesus, and Colosse had some of the same tangents (see 1 Timothy 1:4; Colossians 2:8, 18), including imaginary genealogies of angels. These were needed, so the false teachers said, because believers had to worship angels as well as God. But these speculative arguments took valuable time away from teaching the truth of Scripture and spreading the gospel. POINTLESS CONTROVERSY DOES NOT HELP ADVANCE THE TRUTH. (Caps mine).

Paul warned Titus and Timothy to *avoid* the false teachers' debates and arguments, not even bothering to answer their pretentious positions. This did not mean that the church leaders should refuse to study, discuss, and examine different interpretations of difficult Bible passages. Paul was warning against petty quarrels, not honest discussion that leads to wisdom. As foolish arguments develop, they should rebuke the false teaching (1:13) and turn the discussion back to a helpful and profitable direction. Meanwhile, the faithful minister should continue to emphasize those truths that God wants taught. [32]

Siblings fuss and usually get over it very quickly. Sometimes best friends fuss and they get over it in a matter of days. Co-workers disagree and usually work things out or one is fired and everyone moves on. But, sometimes the

---

[32] *Life Application Bible* Commentary: *1 & 2 Timothy, Titus*, Tyndale, Wheaton, 1991. (Quoted from the software version: WORDsearch Bible, powered by LifeWay.

fuss is not easily resolved and the parties involved go for months, even years without being at peace with other. So, when the fuss or disagreement becomes so destructively intense and demands that the parties compromise their convictions and deny who they really "are," it becomes necessary for them to part ways. When division happens then it ought to be done amiably.

The Apostles who shaped Christianity, beyond the Ascension of Jesus, fussed, and two of them are reported to have "gone separate ways."

> **"Therefore, when Paul and Barnabas had no small dissension and dispute with them, they determined that Paul and Barnabas and certain others of them should go up to Jerusalem, to the apostles and elders, about this question."**
> **(Acts 15:2 NKJV)**

> **"Then the contention became so sharp that they parted from one another. And so Barnabas took Mark and sailed to Cyprus;" (Acts 15:39 NKJV)**

Sometimes the only solution to conflict is parting of ways. Separation from each other is not the best solution – but at times it is the only acceptable solution.

Jesus' disciples argued over things. On one occasion Jesus was having a very special meal with the men who had called to change the world. They were concerned about who would have the most value and the most powerful position in the kingdom. Some of the fussing was over eternal things such as we see in the following passage:

> **Then they began to question among themselves, which of them it was who would do this thing. Now there was also a dispute among them, as to which of them should be considered the greatest. And He said to them, "The kings of the Gentiles exercise lordship over them, and those who exercise authority over them are called 'benefactors.' But not so among you; on the contrary, he who is greatest among you, let him be as the younger, and he who governs as he who serves. For who is greater, he who sits at the table, or he who serves? Is it not he who sits at the table? Yet I am among you as the One who serves. But you are those who have continued with Me in My trials. And I bestow upon you a kingdom, just as My Father bestowed one upon Me, that you may eat and drink at My table in My kingdom, and sit on thrones judging the twelve tribes of Israel." (Luke 22:23-30 NKJV)**

Down through the centuries we humans have experienced yet another principle, many times by simply ignoring it. Solomon wrote: "**The beginning of strife *is like* releasing water; Therefore stop contention before a quarrel starts.**" **Proverbs 17:14 (NKJV)** The dam breaks and destroys everything in its path. The rushing and churning of emotions destroy everything in its path. People are never the same. Dreams are washed away. Hopes are lost. Smiles ride the waves of a bruised countenance.

God can always take those strife-filled experiences and use them for His glory. He has a purpose that is for our good in each of them. Even as I write, I look back and see how God's hand was in each fuss, every conflict and quarrel that I have been a part of. He's teaching, shaping, molding, helping me to take a stand, or die to self in order to make life better not bitter. Out of it all, should come wisdom.

"By pride comes nothing but strife, But with the well-advised *is* wisdom." Proverbs 13:10 (NKJV)

When God birthed the nation of Israel it was not long before the fussing began. We have many examples of the theme of this current chapter. Abraham, the father of the Israelite nation took his nephew Lot with him. Soon there was a fuss over land and possessions. Abram (so he was called early on in the journey, later becoming Abraham) died to self. Abram and Sarai fussed over babies. She could not have a baby early in their marriage. Sarai came up with a plan to give Abram a son. The plan worked. But God did not need Sarai's help. Through her "intervention" into God's plan she caused great problems. That's plural! The relationships of the offspring, Ishmael and Isaac, were strained **which has resulted in turmoil in the Middle East ever since**. Abram failed to stand. Abram had a son by Sarai's handmaid at Sarai's insistence (the root of the turmoil). God later fulfilled His promise to Abram by giving Sarai and Abram a son named Isaac. Through trials and various circumstances, God taught Abraham to stand.

Isaac had two sons, twins but only one of them could receive the inheritance. Their mother Rebekah knew which one was to be heir to the leadership of Israel – Jacob. Rebekah took a stand because of the word that God gave to her while the fighting twins were in her womb.

Jacob fussed with Laban, his father-in-law. Jacob stood and settled for nothing less than what was right.

The battle rages between the Jews and Muslims to this day because of the conflict begun between Abraham's siblings. The fussing spilled over in the 1400's during the Crusades, as Muslims sought to dominate the whole world. Muslims like to blame Christians for that conflict. They are still bitter. The truth is the Crusades were a defense against the exploits of the Muslims who sought to bring their socio-political-theological domination upon all nations in those days. The violence and anarchy that prevailed over much of the world would have continued had it not been for someone taking a stand against this evil. Today, the Radical Muslim factor has picked up the banner and plan jihad and world dominion. They seek to punish the world of infidels - which include EVERYONE who does not bow down to Allah and embrace the Muslim faith and its politics. Islam is a false religion, deceiving its followers regarding eternity and truth in terms of God's (the true God) purpose for individual humans and communities. God is a God of peace except when He must bring judgment upon nations and individuals who refuse to acknowledge Him as their Creator and Master. That is HIS prerogative, not ours. Islam is a prime example of a religious sect that majors on persecution and destruction of people, as their leadership ravages the world, and kills Christians and Jews especially. The Quran (Koran – same book) blatantly advocates this.

Their tactics to dominate the world are clearly seen if one will only read history. They move into a community, a state, or even a nation and begin to populate. They capture a community street by street. Then block by block. Example: Dearborn Michigan. Then when their timing is right, they create confusion, turmoil and chaos. Mostly, they try to disrupt the political system. Sound familiar? What did the Obama administration do? The situation becomes so intense and so threatening that they offer the resolution. They offer peace at their price. If the offer is accepted then they dominate the geographical area. If the offer is denied then they create conflict including military force. Then they dominate. Killing of innocent people and removing the heads of leadership who refuse to follow them is a norm for this radical power across the earth. Muslims now dominate as much as 40% of the continent of Africa. They are quickly moving through Europe – check out Great Britain. The Muslim portion of the world population is 28.26%. [33]

I have a design in this book to help our churches, communities, states and even the nation to recognize the intent of the Evil One to use fussing as a means to destroy us. That is why God has put within my heart such a disdain for arguing and conflict. I share the sentiments of an Old Testament prophet who saw the demise of his nation:

"Why do You show me iniquity, And cause me to see trouble? For plundering and violence are

---

[33] http://www.muslimpopulation.com/World/

before me; There is strife, and contention arises." Habakkuk 1:3 (NKJV)

One of the most powerful influences we face in our nation today is the American Civil Liberties Union (ACLU). It is

> *. . .taking a stand is usually radical!*

neither American nor Civil. It certainly does not protect the liberties of all as it proposes to do. The ACLU uses much of the same tactics as the Muslim leadership. One of the best books to read that exposes the ACLU for all it's worth is *Bad Samaritans*, by Jerome R. Corsi, Ph.D.

Dr. Corsi writes:

> "Since its founding, the ACLU has set out to pervert the First Amendment, written to *preserve* religious freedom, into a twisted interpretation where "freedom *of* religion is now read to mean "freedom *from* religion, a reinterpretation made necessary if the ACLU is to accomplish its long-standing goal of removing God from America's public square."[34]

---

[34] Jerome R. Corsi, *Bad Samaritans*, Nashville, TN. Thomas Nelson, 2013.

144

Maybe we have a word regarding this in the Wisdom literature of the Bible:

"Cast out the scoffer, and contention will leave; Yes, strife and reproach will cease." Proverbs 22:10 (NKJV)

That seems to be radical surgery coming from the King of Wisdom. But, we need to remember that taking a stand is usually radical! Ecclesiastes, (the Preacher) says: "To everything there is a season, A time for every purpose under heaven . . . a time to keep silence and a time to speak;" **(Ecclesiastes 1:1; 7b NKJV)**

In our nation it is a time to STAND.

AMERICA needs to take . . .

. . . The challenge of dying to self and knowing when to stand.

145

Fuss! Fuss! Fuss!

Chapter 9

The Future Fuss

There is coming a close to this age. When I was a student in college my pastor said on a Sunday morning, "One day God is going to step down from glory and say, 'Gentlemen, it's closing time!' "

The stage is being set for the biggest fuss yet among men!

I agree. There has been quite a bit of fussing and warring since the beginning of time as we have seen in the previous chapters. But one day, there will be Peace on Earth and later,

147

peace for eternity. At least as far as "believers in Christ" are concerned! For all others, eternity will be a continual existence of pain, hurting and fussing. Time will be consummated by God, and all those who reject Christ as Lord will be banished to Hell and the Lake of Fire. But we must never forget that the Gospel of Christ proclaims that Christ died for the sins of the world, your sins and my sins. From Adam and Eve to their children, Cain and Able, to the Cross of Jesus, to the Battle of Armageddon, history will record that people have fussed and fumed and fought with each other and with God.

The Great Enemy of the cross is behind all of this feuding and fussing because <u>the one thing that generates fussing is sin.</u> Satan is the Great Enemy – of God, of God's people and even the unbeliever. The source of all evil is Satan. He is also called Lucifer. He was an archangel, who led a rebellion in Heaven, was "thrown out of Heaven" and is known in the Bible as the EVIL ONE (See Isaiah 14 for background). The Devil, Satan, The Evil One, the Father of Lies, all names of THE arch enemy of Christians, has been starting fusses ever since that rebellion. He came to Adam and Eve in the Garden of Eden and tempted them to sin and thus, because of their yielding to sin, fussing began on earth. Have you

148

ever heard a child questioned by a parent when something was done that was not in keeping with the family's values? The response sometimes is: "Billy made me do it!" [put your own chosen name in the place of "Billy."] Now, hear Adam speaking to God about his sin. "Eve made me do it!" How do you think that made Eve feel? Did Adam just not know that God is all-knowing (omniscient)?

But, God is going to put an end to this activity; and when he does, and the believers are taken out of this world – oh the fussing! Who gets what? Everything we leave behind – money, clothes, land, even some children, will be up for grabs. The one with the most power will get it. But, then, even more fussing erupts. The apocalyptic literature describes it.

Daniel describes this time in the last chapter of the book named for him. He says:

> **1 "At that time Michael shall stand up, The great prince who stands watch over the sons of your people; And there shall be a time of trouble, Such as never was since there was a nation, Even to that time. And at that time your people shall be delivered, Every one who is found written in the book.**

2 And many of those who sleep in the dust of the earth shall awake, Some to everlasting life, Some to shame and everlasting contempt.
7 Then I heard the man clothed in linen, who was above the waters of the river, when he held up his right hand and his left hand to heaven, and swore by Him who lives forever, that it shall be for a time, times, and half a time; and when the power of the holy people has been completely shattered, all these things shall be finished.
(Daniel 12:1-2, NKJV)

Ezekiel is one of the major prophets of the Old Testament period. He describes this future event like this: (God speaking)

21 "I will set My glory among the nations; all the nations shall see My judgment which I have executed, and My hand which I have laid on them.
22 So the house of Israel shall know that I am the LORD their God from that day forward.
23 The Gentiles shall know that the house of Israel went into captivity for their iniquity; because they were unfaithful to Me, therefore I hid My face from them. I gave them into the hand of their enemies, and they all fell by the sword.
24 According to their uncleanness and according to their transgressions I have dealt with them, and hidden My face from them." '
25 "Therefore thus says the Lord GOD: 'Now I will bring back the captives of Jacob, and have

> mercy on the whole house of Israel; and I will be
> jealous for My holy name--
> 26 after they have borne their shame, and all
> their unfaithfulness in which they were
> unfaithful to Me, when they dwelt safely in their
> own land and no one made them afraid.
> 27 When I have brought them back from the
> peoples and gathered them out of their enemies'
> lands, and I am hallowed in them in the sight of
> many nations,
> 28 then they shall know that I am the LORD
> their God, who sent them into captivity among
> the nations, but also brought them back to their
> land, and left none of them captive any longer.
> 29 And I will not hide My face from them
> anymore; for I shall have poured out My Spirit
> on the house of Israel,' says the Lord GOD."
> (Ezekiel 39:21-29 NKJV)

Paul, the Apostle, in writing to the church at Thessalonica addressed the question that concerned the believers, "What will happen to those of us who believe and have died or will die?" They were looking for Christ to return in their lifetime. Some were so confused about this that they simply quit working and sat down to wait on the big event. Paul corrected this misconception by providing the truth regarding the doctrine of eschatology.

Part of that explanation follows:

> 13 But I do not want you to be ignorant,
> brethren, concerning those who have fallen

asleep, lest you sorrow as others who have no hope.

14 For if we believe that Jesus died and rose again, even so God will bring with Him those who sleep in Jesus.

15 For this we say to you by the word of the Lord, that we who are alive and remain until the coming of the Lord will by no means precede those who are asleep.

16 For the Lord Himself will descend from heaven with a shout, with the voice of an archangel, and with the trumpet of God. And the dead in Christ will rise first.

17 Then we who are alive and remain shall be caught up together with them in the clouds to meet the Lord in the air. And thus we shall always be with the Lord.

18 Therefore comfort one another with these words (1 Thessalonians 4:13-18 (NKJV).

I have included an "Events of the Last Days" chart in the Appendix.

The Church is made up of believers in Christ.

The period to consummate the life of humankind on earth is called "the seven years of Tribulation." Just before those seven years, a huge event called by many theologians "the Rapture" will take place. This is the extraction of the

Church, from the Earth as seen in the passage above. The Church includes all believers in Jesus Christ who have experienced redemption through faith by grace. Everyone who says they are a "member of the church" (or A church in particular) will not necessarily be raptured since many "members" are not Christians. They are like, even the devil himself. Satan believes that Jesus is the Christ because he knows Christ is real, but he trembles (James 2:19). True believers will experience what is called the "Rapture of the Church."

Now let me unpack the terms that I have just used, in sequential order, to describe this "future fuss." **First, is the Rapture of the Church.** I must be candid here. There are theologians who do not believe this is a true doctrine of the Bible, because the word is not used, or because they interpret prophecy and apocalyptic literature differently. Nonetheless, I have studied the Scriptures thoroughly and hold to the belief that the Church, which metaphorically is called the Body, the Bride and the Building of Christ, will be taken out of this world before the Great Tribulation. In like manner, the word "Trinity" is not found in the Bible. But I believe in the Trinity, because of the overwhelming evidence that God the Father, God the Son and God the Holy Spirit,

153

all manifested persons of God are found in the Bible and in the reality, of life. He is One Person manifested in three ways. The Holy Spirit is not an "it" like you would talk about the "spirit" of St. Louis. "The Spirit of St. Louis" IS an IT. The trinity is three Persons of the Godhead, manifested to humans in different forms. So, the Holy Spirit is not an it! He lives. He works. He abides. He is present in the believer.

So, there is the teaching that the Church will be "caught up together in the air" – a moment when Christ comes for them, and then later returns, visibly and in all power to set up His earthly kingdom. In 1 Thessalonians 4:17 Paul uses the words "caught up together" to describe the time when Christ returns for His Church. That is the phrase for the doctrinal belief of the "rapture." The silent evidence is seen in the book of Revelation. In chapters one through three, the church is seen on Earth. Chapter four opens with a scene in Heaven, and the reader never sees the Church again on the earth in remaining words of *The Revelation*. What happens to the Church during this apocalyptic period? The Church is raptured. Only the Church is raptured. Unbelievers are left in this world for a short time. They will die in the seven-year period of the Tribulation, or at the end. Those who are not believers and died as such, are in Hell and will be raised at the end of time for their final Judgment as they stand before God at the Great White Throne.

The Church is made up of believers in Christ. Those who "receive" Christ, that is make a personal choice to take the free gift of eternal life from God, accept what Christ has done in His Life and in his death as atonement for

> **But the end of all things is at hand; therefore be serious and watchful in your prayers.**
> **(1 Peter 4:7 (NKJV)**

one's own sin, and believe that He was raised from the dead, are the elect of God, the family of God, and will be raptured to spend eternity with Christ in glory. In the text above, Daniel alludes to those whose names are written in the book whereas; John clarifies this "list" for us. Those written in the Book are all the people who were ever born (or supposed to be born, but were not birthed due to a medical condition or because of sin perpetrated upon an innocent soul, such as abortion). Those written in the Lamb's Book of Life are those who have received Christ and His atoning blood sacrifice for their sin.

Second, is the Seven Years of Tribulation. It is not the scope of this volume to discuss in detail the beliefs that abound regarding the Tribulation – "Pre-Trib;" "Post-Trib;" "Mid-Trib;" or no-Trib. Tribulation is being prepared now on the world stage. I see it in the Muslim takeover of nations, and the emergence of the Communist Party of China. It was seen in the fifties and sixties with a Communist takeover of the world. Muslims, communists, fascists and other such political aberrations in the world may be stopped in our day just as God stopped the Babylonians, the Assyrians, the Persians, the Romans and other such powers down through history. But the key component in "future things" is to understand what God does with Israel. Israel is the thermometer to read the temperature of God's Climatic Activity. Israel is the "fig tree" that Jesus referred to in Matthew 24:32.

The Tribulation can be broken into two parts – The first three and one-half years and the second three and one-half years. Neither the Church nor the Holy Spirit will be present on the Earth during this time. Hence, all evil and immorality will multiply and be focused on destroying "Israel, God's timepiece," as it has been called by many. The Tribulation, and the second half of the tribulation, known as the GREAT tribulation, will be a time for everything to escalate and speed up. The Revelation portrays this truth as the reader sees death, disease, demonic activity and Devil domination intensify. Time runs out for the Evil One, which causes him to make things happen as just described.

The stage is being set for the biggest fuss yet among men. Students of the Word of God can see this clearly. It is not quite so clear to the unbeliever, the non-Christian world of academics, anti-God social media, and the like. Politics plays a huge role in this setup. God is using national "rulers" and "key people of the nations" to prepare for the coming of Christ. Time nor space does not allow me to include in this volume all that needs to be said for perfect understanding of the times we live in. However, a few examples will give you, the reader, an idea.

Israel is God's timepiece. Israel became a recognized nation once again in 1948. Many of us see this as the prophecy Jesus spoke in Matthew 24, when He said:

3 Now as He sat on the Mount of Olives, the disciples came to Him privately, saying, "Tell us,

when will these things be? And what will be the sign of Your coming, and of the end of the age?"
4 And Jesus answered and said to them: "Take heed that no one deceives you.
5 For many will come in My name, saying, 'I am the Christ,' and will deceive many.
6 And you will hear of wars and rumors of wars. See that you are not troubled; for all these things must come to pass, but the end is not yet.
7 For nation will rise against nation, and kingdom against kingdom. And there will be famines, pestilences, and earthquakes in various places.
8 All these are the beginning of sorrows.
9 Then they will deliver you up to tribulation and kill you, and you will be hated by all nations for My name's sake.
10 And then many will be offended, will betray one another, and will hate one another.
11 Then many false prophets will rise up and deceive many.
12 And because lawlessness will abound, the love of many will grow cold.
13 But he who endures to the end shall be saved.
14 And this gospel of the kingdom will be preached in all the world as a witness to all the nations, and then the end will come.
15 "Therefore when you see the 'abomination of desolation,' spoken of by Daniel the prophet, standing in the holy place" (whoever reads, let him understand),
16 then let those who are in Judea flee to the mountains.
17 Let him who is on the housetop not go down to take anything out of his house.

18 And let him who is in the field not go back to get his clothes.

19 But woe to those who are pregnant and to those who are nursing babies in those days!

20 And pray that your flight may not be in winter or on the Sabbath.

21 For then there will be great tribulation, such as has not been since the beginning of the world until this time, no, nor ever shall be.

22 And unless those days were shortened, no flesh would be saved; but for the elect's sake those days will be shortened.

23 Then if anyone says to you, 'Look, here is the Christ!' or 'There!' do not believe it.

24 For false christs and false prophets will rise and show great signs and wonders to deceive, if possible, even the elect.

25 See, I have told you beforehand.

26 Therefore if they say to you, 'Look, He is in the desert!' do not go out; or 'Look, He is in the inner rooms!' do not believe it.

27 For as the lightning comes from the east and flashes to the west, so also will the coming of the Son of Man be.

28 For wherever the carcass is, there the eagles will be gathered together.

29 "Immediately after the tribulation of those days the sun will be darkened, and the moon will not give its light; the stars will fall from heaven, and the powers of the heavens will be shaken.

30 Then the sign of the Son of Man will appear in heaven, and then all the tribes of the earth will mourn, and they will see the Son of Man coming on the clouds of heaven with power and great glory.

31 And He will send His angels with a great sound of a trumpet, and they will gather together His elect from the four winds, from one end of heaven to the other. (Matthew 24:3-31 NKJV)

There will be no CHURCH to balance the words or decisions.

The disciples of Jesus asked their Master to tell them when the end of the world would come. Jesus did not tell them "Stop asking such questions!" or "Don't try to understand the consummation of the ages." Rather, he laid out for them some very important principles about understanding the way God the Father is going to wrap things up. There was no scolding in the message of Jesus as he tells them some things of the future. He did not say you do not need to worry about such things. No, He clearly answered their question and gave them the plan of the Father in a nutshell. Using the story of a fig tree, Jesus clearly helped the disciples to know something of the future of their nation and the world. The "Fig tree"(v32) is Israel.

32 "Now learn this parable from the fig tree:
When its branch has already become tender and
puts forth leaves, you know that summer is near.
33 So you also, when you see all these things,
know that it is near--at the doors!
34 Assuredly, I say to you, this generation will
by no means pass away till all these things take
place.
35 Heaven and earth will pass away, but My
words will by no means pass away.
36 "But of that day and hour no one knows, not
even the angels of heaven, but My Father only.
37 But as the days of Noah were, so also will the
coming of the Son of Man be.
38 For as in the days before the flood, they were
eating and drinking, marrying and giving in
marriage, until the day that Noah entered the
ark,
39 and did not know until the flood came and
took them all away, so also will the coming of the
Son of Man be.
40 Then two men will be in the field: one will be
taken and the other left.
41 Two women will be grinding at the mill: one
will be taken and the other left.
42 Watch therefore, for you do not know what
hour your Lord is coming.
43 But know this, that if the master of the house
had known what hour the thief would come, he
would have watched and not allowed his house to
be broken into.
44 Therefore you also be ready, for the Son of
Man is coming at an hour you do not expect.
45 "Who then is a faithful and wise servant,
whom his master made ruler over his household,
to give them food in due season?

161

**46 Blessed is that servant whom his master,
when he comes, will find so doing.
47 Assuredly, I say to you that he will make him
ruler over all his goods.
48 But if that evil servant says in his heart, 'My
master is delaying his coming,'
49 and begins to beat his fellow servants, and to
eat and drink with the drunkards,
50 the master of that servant will come on a day
when he is not looking for him and at an hour
that he is not aware of,
51 and will cut him in two and appoint him his
portion with the hypocrites. There shall be
weeping and gnashing of teeth (Matthew 24:32-
51 NKJV).**

Also note the battle over oil. The whole Middle East is in
conflict because of their "oil." Oil plays a major role in the
end times. Oil is a major topic of discussion in politics
today. Talk radio and TV hosts discuss the ramifications of
the oil supply. Many believe most of the wars that have been
fought in the last one hundred years were over oil. Consider
the governments of Saudi Arabia, Iraq, Iran, and other
Middle Eastern countries, along with Venezuela, and other
South American countries. These national leaders, mostly
dictatorial, control other nations by the supply of oil. The
words being screamed by these nations: "Death to America"
and "Death to all the Jews!" – are simply symptoms of
bigger issues. The populace of these countries does not

understand the role the United States plays in keeping peace around the world. Some say however, that the United States cannot continue to be the "Policeman of the world." I agree. But, we still need to stand with our friends in other countries in order to stamp out evil where we can, militarily, politically, socially, and economically. In addition, the church is mandated to attack the gates of evil with full force. The Body of Christ uses different weapons - love, prayer, service, kindness and lifestyles that change hearts.

HOT SPOTS AROUND THE WORLD TOAY 2022

As I revise this book, I searched what some consider the political hotspots around the world. The searh was almost futile. Most of the writing is slanted LEFT. It is typical of the public media today. I was saddened. I think it is safe to assume that every nation in the world will in 2022 face trouble, disease, tyranny, threats of war, hunger, sexual abuse, mistreatment of women, political unrest, and much more.

Protestors will show up. Sometimes they are legitimate; sometimes not. People will continue to be killed for their beliefs. Just review some recent past events and change the names a bit and you get a picture of what will happen in the next three years. At home we saw/see scandal after political scandal:

- The IRS coming down like Gestapo on Christian businesses.
- NPR (public radio which cannot be trusted with truth)
- The EPA is hostile to free enterprise and especially in places toward faith-based organizations.
- Ben Carson, a top respected neuro surgeon as candidate for the presidency saw first hand the ugly side of liberal politics.
- Hobby Lobby won a gigantic fuss over insurance in the fiasco created by "Obama Care."
- Duck Dynasty found themselves in a huge fuss over issues regarding religion and homosexuality.
- The government of the USA is using computers to dig into the personal lives of millions of its citizens, unethically and illegally. And if you go to get a vaccination for Covid, they ask tons of questions that are frankly NON OF THEIR BUSINES.
- The IRS, reportedly compromised sixty (60) million records of US citizens.

- Allegedly, government officials in 2013, were caught prying into the medical business of individuals.

- A big fuss has erupted over the January 6, 2021 event at the Capitol and the blame is placed on President Trump who certainly would not condone such actions.

- The man who was in the White House before Trump created a fuss over a deserter by name of Bergdahl.

- The White House created a fuss over food served to children at school. Where is that in the Constitution?

- Muslims show up on top of the reservoir in Boston.

- Hillary runs for president and no sooner than she visits a key state to begin campaigning, it is revealed that she has taken millions of dollars from countries, deemed our enemies. It is reported that she has secretly sold our security for millions of dollars to be placed in the Clinton Foundation.

- Democrats steal a national election and a liberal Supreme Court is too weak to take action.

News people are fussing over the correct way to handle all these crises. Politicians are fussing about who's in control.

Europe is on brink of takeover by Muslims. This book seeks to provide:

Hope,

Encouragement,

Comfort,

and some handles on how to begin winning over the debilitating issues of a fuss.

One World Government is emerging. It could be Sharia law if the Muslims win the day. Most Muslims currently living in the United States believe that their Sharia law takes precedence over the constitution of the United States of America. What if citizens of the United States of America moved to a Muslim country and demanded or insisted or purported that our Holy Bible supersedes the Sharia law of that country? How long would you or I be able to live? How the United States fits into this scheme is still up for grabs.

That may be why not much evidence is in the Bible about the United States being a world power during the period of the Great Tribulation and beyond. The United States may be what Biblical writers alluded to as "the islands being removed." (See Revelation 6:14 and 16:20) John knew nothing about nuclear warfare, but he described what he saw and we have seen a bit of how that truly and literally can happen. Why would the United States Congress and the Pentagon keep silent over a president giving $1.5 billion (with a B) to Iran? What guarantee do we have that this will not buy the nuclear muscle and technology to literally annihilate the United States?

Look at the Education conflict. It is moving ever closer to the anti-God, evolutionary mindset that destroys the faith of young students. In 2015, our nation was in a battle over the educational nightmare called "COMMON CORE" which will destroy the education system of the United States. It will also be an economic nightmare. True spiritual wisdom is left out of this philosophy of education. WE need to stand against any politician or movement that supports common core. It serves to "dumb down" our children's education. Now we are faced with CRITICAL RACE THEORY.

It is . . .

. . . The challenge of dying to self and knowing when to stand.

167

Fuss! Fuss! Fuss!

Chapter 10

Standing for the Future

Jesus is coming soon!

As we STAND, we need to have a deep understanding of God's Word. The Bible gives us the wisdom, insight, and power to face the coming catastrophe. As Jesus looked in a forward direction He told His Church that we can overcome. We are overcomers as we know God's Word, apply the blood of Christ to our hearts, and do not love our life even to death. Future events shape our present behavior. If we know that there are consequences in the future based on our decisions and actions in the present, whether it is a reward or a regret, we just might be persuaded to go for the reward. That is the value of true prophecy.

You see, we are on the verge of experiencing the power and presence of the Anti-Christ. Therefore,

I want to move ahead in this chapter to understand the future scheme of events. Then as I close out, we can back up to the present in order for us to get the feel for the seriousness of standing for our faith today. Only when we can see the end will we be motivated to do something in the present. I know when I was in my late teens and into my twenties it was constantly on my mind. I wanted to be sure that I would not be a part of this coming earthly tribulation. And, you can too.

The fuss will rage. We don't know when these events will take place. But, after the Rapture of the Church, that is, the removal of Christian believers (the Born-Again) from the Earth, which happens as recorded between the events of chapters three and four of *The Revelation*, there will be no church to balance the words spoken by those in control, or the decisions made by a godless world. There will be no presence of the Holy Spirit, as He will be withdrawn from the Earth. God begins to pour out His wrath upon a world misled by Satan. The Great Creator becomes the Great Consummator. Again, as one reads the book of Revelation, beyond chapter three, he sees that the church is no longer on the earth. Then, as the reader moves on to Revelation 6:1, the reader sees who will stand on the earth.

The scene quickly shifts from worship in chapter five to wrath in chapter six. God's wrath upon a sin-sick world rides in on four

The Great Creator becomes the Great Consummator.

symbolic horses. However, this symbolism is in reality the wrath of God! The horsemen and their horses are introduced by thunder, which easily gets one's attention. The hoof beats have been heard by the occupants of earth for decades before they arrive.

171

Only those who listened carefully heard them coming and prepared themselves. John the Apostle heard it and saw it and wrote it down for us to know and understand. Dwight L. Moody heard them. So did Billy Sunday, and Billy Graham and in our current culture David Jeremiah, Robert Jeffries, and a host of evangelical, conservative, Bible-believing pastors along with countless numbers of the Laity. Do you hear them?

John gives his readers many symbols and signs in groups of seven. One of those series of sevens is the seals. Each seal opens to the next one. When the seventh seal is opened it becomes the next series of sevens,

There will be no church to balance the words or decisions the world makes.

which are angels blowing trumpets. The trumpets sound and the seventh become figures, and the seventh figure becomes bowls.

We see in this chapter the struggle between God and the Devil. We see people in their destiny; their decision. These people decided to have it their way, to do it their way, to reject the only one who could give them eternal life – Jesus. Man, without Christ, is not a victim of wrong thinking, wrong planning, wrong circumstances, nor a wrong calendar. But he is a victim of the DEVIL, just as Peter the apostle said, "He [Satan] is a roaring lion, seeking whom he may devour. The Anti-Christ is the person who will govern the world for a short time. Scholars know that this happens during what Daniel, the Prophet, called the Seventieth (70th) week" as recorded in his prophetic writing.

Daniel 9:20-27 (SEE chart in appendix)

In the timeline of history, as the Old Testament prophet Daniel explains it; and as some of us understand it, there are three periods of time termed as weeks. There is a total of seventy (70) weeks. These are weeks of years. That is, you and I know and speak of a week as seven DAYS. But, God is counting time in **YEARS** as He gives Daniel this prophecy. The total time being considered is 490 years – (7 the number of a week; and 70 the number of weeks, thus 7 X 70 = 490). The first period is one week of forty-nine (49) years and relates to the time that describes the decree for Nehemiah to rebuild the walls of Jerusalem in 445 B.C. The second segment which relates to the sixty-two (62) weeks of years (434 years) described the time that passes after Nehemiah till the Messiah was cut off, which alludes to the life and ministry of Jesus the Christ (Messiah) and His crucifixion. Both of these periods (483 years) have passed and only one (1) week (seven years) remains. The third period is the SEVENTIETH WEEK OF DANIEL (7 years). That totals 490 years as the prophecy states. This last week is not back to back with the other 69 weeks, since Christ died almost two thousand years ago. This period is the TIMES OF THE GENTILES.

Other names used for the SEVENTIETH WEEK period found in the Scriptures are:
1. The Time of Jacob's trouble
2. Time, times and half a time
3. 1260 days, or 42 months

Other passages of Scripture used to understand this time period are: Matthew 24; Mark 13; Luke 21.

It is "the time of Jacob's trouble," which is one concept of how the tribulation is described in prophecy. Therefore, what is seen as a symbolic event in prophecy, becomes a

174

historical event in reality. The symbolism of the White Horse with a bow is in reality a person who is Anti-Christ – alive, human, powerful and evil. And, anti-God! The world waits for a "person" to unite the powers and peoples of the earth. He will be Satan's counterfeit in a globalism of evil and a New World Order.

The Anti-Christ sells himself as a person of peace. However, he only comes to TAKE peace from the earth. He brings terror, bloodshed, war and death. Greedy men won't care about wives and children. Greedy, stupid, sinful men like most of the dictators in our world of yesterday and today will kill wildlife and jeopardize the future of the nations of the world. Death reigns for a while. Necessities of life become scarce. Earthquakes happen in magnitudinal proportions. Millions of people die. Nature goes crazy. The Sun and Moon are darkened, possibly from the vapor and smoke brought about by explosions and earthquakes. Stars that have orbited in space for centuries suddenly fall from the sky. It is the End of the World as we know it.

> *Now, let's come back to the present by way of the first century A.D.*
>
> *(I am avoiding the word Circa, preferring the Latin: Anno Domini = "in the year of our Lord".)*

We have words from the Apostle Paul that we ought to heed in these days prior to the Second Coming of Christ. Dying to Self is Biblical. See the truth in Colossians 3:5-9 which says:

> ⁴ **When Christ *who is* our life appears, then you also will appear with Him in glory.**
> ⁵ **Therefore put to death your members which are on the earth: fornication, uncleanness, passion, evil desire, and covetousness, which is idolatry.**
> ⁶ **Because of these things the wrath of God is coming upon the sons of disobedience,**
> ⁷ **in which you yourselves once walked when you lived in them.**
> ⁸ **But now you yourselves are to put off all these: anger, wrath, malice, blasphemy, filthy language out of your mouth.**
> ⁹ **Do not lie to one another, since you have put off the old man with his deeds," (Colossians 3:4-9 NKJV).**

False teachers are being addressed by Paul. So, today, we are experiencing the same thing as we see our universities filled with teachers who are not telling students the truth. Students come out of these universities with philosophies and knowledge that do not line up with THE truth.

Therefore, it spills over into our homes, our businesses, the marketplace and our churches. We are living in a world (at least in advanced civilized world) where everyone must have their

Dying to self is Biblical!

"rights" and the minority rules. Christians sometimes behave just like the world. It is time for the church to learn better.

A few years ago, scholars began to introduce a term: "WOKE" and it has dominated media and academia. Wokeness is nothing more than a ploy to destroy everything that is wholesome and right and yes every historical thing that doesn't fit in with their liberal agenda. Many pastors are making a terrible mistake of leading their churches into "wokeness." Thus they are loosing their witness, their ministry to a world in desperate need of the true Gospel. In our own convention many leaders have embarrassed themselves and removed "their candlestick" because they became woke.

The scripture above gives us guidance in learning to "die to self" and obtaining freedom from those things that cause fussing. Francis Dixon share's in his *Bible Study Notes:*

> *"May the mind of Christ my Saviour*
> *Live in me from day to day,*
> *By His love and pow'r controlling*
> *All I do and say."[35]*

The hoof beats are loudly calling us to beware of coming calamity. And, the sound of thunder is on the horizon, today! I will never forget one Wednesday night we were at church, where I served as pastor in Florida. We were finishing our church supper, and someone came to the fellowship hall and announced: "It's begun!" In the mind of everyone around Hurlburt AFB, we knew what that meant. The Desert Shield had become the Desert Storm.

---

[35] Francis Dixon, *Bible Study Notes,* Word of Life Ministries, 4/5 Regency Mews, Eastbourne BN20 7AB, England, Series Eleven, Study 6.

Our men were some of the first in. Our Air Force helicopters went in to raise the radar detection devices. Behind those were our jet fighters which knocked their radar out so that more aircraft could get in. The rest is history. What a battle - and you saw it in living color in your den or living room. Some of us wondered if this could be the day the church would be raptured. We weren't but the day could still be close at hand. The stage is being set for Revelation six to be fulfilled.

John uses symbolism, and much of it military. The lamb prevailed to open the seals. John turns the readers' attention from the beauty and grandeur of Heaven to the perplexing and catastrophic scenes of EARTH during the Tribulation. What you saw in Desert Storm and later in the Gulf War previews that time which is yet to come.

In this day, most politicians are but pawns in the hands of Satan, putting together something they believe will be best for the world. But, in reality, according to the Bible these government officials are setting the stage for Armageddon, the last fuss and the last battle in the world.

Before the Tribulation, however, Christians will be persecuted as never before. The Church will need to stand for the FAITH. You and I will need to be equipped to STAND against all of Satan's tactics and attacks. What will cause the evil of the world to retreat and ultimately be defeated? In the present, Christians can unite in ways to carry the Gospel to the whole world. Christians can engage the culture as they also lovingly confront the culture. Christians can trust God to work in this world on their behalf as they are obedient to follow Him. One day a "Posse" of gigantic proportion will arrive on the scene in this world – Jesus and His host of angels and the saints whom He has redeemed – and King Jesus will rule and reign – even from Jerusalem!

Photographer Nichole Cambre was on assignment on an island which is in the middle of the Chobe River, near Botswana, in Africa. She saw a hippopotamus whose territory was being invaded by an African elephant. The elephant had crossed the river and the hippo was growing angry. It felt compelled to defend its territory. The hippo showed his teeth as he moved in on the elephant. Getting close to the elephant he did not back down until other elephants showed up. The elephants had confidence their

BIGNESS would win the day, and it did as the hippo went back into the river.[36]

Sometimes we have to stand alone. It is best if we stand together in unity. We can make a difference by supporting each other. The above illustration fails to be perfect, since it is a story of nature. But, when it comes to human relationships we must stand and be faithful to what is true, moral, and pleasing to God.

Again, we are looking at Revelation, Chapter six (6) for insight regarding the Final Fuss! Here are a few observations to consider clarifying this prophecy and enabling you to see how God is at work in the present to bring our fussing to a Grand Finale.

Verse One: When a heavenly matter is addressed it is the elders who speak. When an earthly matter is addressed, it is the creatures who speak.

Verse Two: The White horse is not to be mistaken for Christ. It is the Anti-Christ or the power of the Anti-Christ

---

[36] http://www.foxnews.com/science/2013/10/04/hippo-vs-elephant-animal-giants-face-off/

to make War, thus the bow. Although the white horse
symbolizes peace, and that is what is promised, this
individual ushers in the deadliest times in the history of
mankind. Think of the "nations" today and their symbols.
Here are just a few. The Bear is a symbol of Russian. The
Bald Eagle is a symbol of The United States of America. The
Lion represents Great Britain. The cycle and hammer
represent communism. The Star and Crescent is a symbol for
Islam.

The whole scene is one of judgment. Paul says in Romans
8:22-25:
> **"For we know that the whole creation groans
> and labors with birth pangs together until now
> . . . we ourselves groan within ourselves, eagerly
> waiting for the adoption, the redemption or our
> body. For we were saved in this hope . . . for
> what we do not see, we eagerly wait for it with
> perseverance."**

Nature itself has "an awareness," a God-given sense of
knowing, that all is not well. Nature, including everything,
even the mountains, the oceans, the weather, speak today of
a great strain that it is under and longs for redemption, for
salvation, for renewal.   Jesus will come and make that
happen. For His highest creation – MAN – that means a
FAITH RELATIONSHIP WITH GOD THROUGH JESUS

CHRIST WILL RESULT IN COMPLETE REDEMPTION
FROM A FALLEN WORLD OF SIN. One who does not
have that relationship will experience complete and final
judgment as God's wrath is poured out upon this world.

I'm sure John was familiar with Zechariah's prophecy. That
Old Testament spokesman for God used similar imagery as
he declared judgment upon Babylon and Egypt (Zechariah
6:1-8) The crown that John saw was a crown of victory,
representing the power given to the Anti-Christ who will be
allowed to conquer nations. The world today waits for a man
to unite the nations. He could be living as I write and as you
read this book. He will be Satan's counterfeit. He will have
mindset to conquer the globe. It is ultimately a New World
Order.

Verses Three and Four: War (conflict)
Here is the real purpose of the Anti-Christ. He comes in as a
peacemaker but really comes to take peace from the world.
After all, he is opposed to everything Christ stands for. And,
Christ is the Prince of Peace. Note that the Anti-Christ will
"take peace from the earth," and that peace will be replaced
with global conflict, even in places like the United States of
America where unrest and violence continue to grow until

the whole nation is fussing with each other. Then, WAR breaks out. The red horse shows up. Red symbolizes the terror, bloodshed, war, death that is part of this Tribulation period. (See also: 6:3-5; 12:3; 17:3) In order to get a fuller picture, one must also look at Ezekiel 38 – 39. Russia and its allies are symbolically described as using "great swords" the emblem of war and slaughter. A quick look at Daniel 11:40ff will give more insight as to the war that's coming.

Verses Five and Six: Famine

In these verses we learn that there will be great famine upon the earth. During this famine the Anti-Christ will insist on a way to control who gets the resources to survive. John calls it the mark of the beast (Revelation 13:16-17). Things of necessity get scarce. The land has been destroyed. Listen to the description of money being used today. Billions and Trillions. When one project in our government today costs billions of dollars for a three-month operation, ask yourself "How many could that feed?" Where is the leader in our day like Joseph? Just take note of the waste in our world today. Look at the Endowment of the arts -what a waste! Note Planned Parenthood which harvests baby parts to resell, and is funded by taxpayer dollars. And, there are many more. Is that NOT the world groaning for redemption? Look at the luxuries, the plentiful, the abundance that is used for frivolous things, while necessities are scarce to so many. And, just to clarify, I'm not talking socialism here. I'm not in agreement of taking from the rich to feed the poor. Forcing people to give is not Biblical. Rather we are to teach people to get up, get a job and provide through work what the individual and his or her family needs.

There will be a time when "a quart of wheat will require a day's wages." Remember I told you about shopping for the first time with Patricia when we were just married. I have left "most" of the buying of groceries to her. The other day she was out of town and there was not "bread" in the house. She suggested I go to a "FRED's" and pick up a loaf. I did. Man, was I shocked! I paid $3.89 for a loaf of bread. I had not bought any bread for years. I could not believe it! I thought: "Wow! I used to make $1.25 an hour when I graduated from High School. That's three hours of work. Of course, when I told Patricia about my purchase, she reassured me that I could have gotten my bread form the PIGGLY WIGGLY for under two dollars. But the time is coming!

We are almost there. I had to buy a two by four today. It cost me $4.98 – one pine stick called a 2" X 4" X 8'. Only five years ago one could purchase them all day long for ninety-eight cents.

When that time comes, greedy men won't care about wives and children. Greedy, stupid, sinful men and women, like Saddam Hussein, ISSIS leaders, and others, will kill the wildlife and jeopardize the future of the world. They will behave just like old Ahab and Jezebel who jeopardized the whole Arab / Jewish world by their selfishness (I Kings).

Verse Seven: Pale - death

The final horse we look at is DEATH, but it is not the FINALE! These are simply signs of the end. John used a word – "behold" which means a startling sight. What did he see? It was the Grim Reaper - who has now come on the scene taking lives in a multitude of ways. However, we need to look all the way through with eyes of faith and see what happens in chapter 20:14. The whole world will be shaken. Millions will die. Remember, millions have been extracted at the Rapture. But in the short months after the Rapture, the world will experience chaos. Will you be ready for the

Rapture and avoid this calamity? How about your family and friends? Tell them about Jesus today.

The truth is DEATH is not the end to human life. The Good News is that Christians live forever through Christ who conquered death for us (Romans 5:12-20). Between rapture and the **REVELATION** (the Second Coming) of Christ – death rides unbridled (Matthew 24:22). Death was defeated on the cross. Death will be deleted at the Great White Throne (I Corinthians 15:26). The sting of death has been removed for the Believer NOW! We do not have to fear death.

A full one-fourth of the world (which is the largest number ever to die at once) will die. It could be possibly atomic, or hydrogen, nuclear, or chemical. It might be a virus. If "parrot fever" in one cubic centimeter of mass can infect twenty (20) million people, think about the combination of all these causes of death. Think about all the "tests" being done with COVID viruses. Is it population control setting in? The three other horses had one instrument of judgment. The fourth has four means of judgment: sword, hunger, death – pestilence, and beasts. **(See: Matthew 24: 3-14)**

Oh, wait, didn't we just experience a once in a lifetime epidemic called Covid 19. Does that really mean as someone suggested?

C = certificate; O = of; V = validation; 19 = 2019?

Are we getting close? I have made many a medical office registration person, or nurse mad at me simply because I refuse to have my temperature checked on my forehead. They will do it on my wrist or not at all. Do you see what is happening? The government and political leaders are preparing us by innocently asking us to participate in "a new way of doing an old thing," for the mark of the beast.

People will be hardened. I know that personally: While pastoring in Georgia, I encountered a man sitting on his porch. I was making an evangelistic visit. He was an alcoholic and he was bitter. As I visited him I just kinda loved on him, with the love of Christ. I found out he had a son who was killed in Viet Nam. In the conversation I shared with him that God had a son to die in the greatest war of all. That resonated with him and the man received Christ. God took away the bitterness and the sin of alcohol use. He became a man faithful to God.

In the rest of Revelation, Chapter Six, we see the souls
martyred for their faith in Christ during the tribulation.
Martyrs before this time period were all "raptured." We see
pictures from the Old Testament sacrificial system with the
blood poured out under the altar. These martyrs repudiated
the anti-Christ (Matthew 24:9-10). God's not done at this
point. The rest of the book of Revelation will reveal God's
plan for total judgment upon sin and Satan. God rearranges
things.

Deliverance is not through an idea, nor a philosophy, but a
person -- Jesus Christ, the Lamb of God. Through Christ we
can move from being victims to being VICTORS! We move
from tragedy to TRIUMPH! This book seeks to provide:
Hope, Encouragement, Comfort.

Therefore, be diligent in . . .

. . . The challenge of dying to self and knowing when to stand.

Fuss! Fuss! Fuss!

Chapter 11

The Flight from Fussing

Denying self is a gigantic task. We don't really like to do it. We fight it. Self wants to sit on the throne of our hearts ALL THE TIME. In, *Telling Yourself the Truth*, the authors Backus and Chapian write:

> "Sometimes it is not easy to deny yourself. It's not easy to go without something you desperately want, not easy to give up something you dearly prize, not easy to lose something you cherish. BUT, sometimes for the sake of a higher, more noble life, it's necessary. Most of the time, in fact, you'll find that gaining something valuable in your life will depend on being willing to tolerate distress, anxiety,

discomfort and discontent. Your greatest achievements are often won because you are willing to put up with situations which are often downright unpleasant."[37]

No wonder God declares: *"He who is* slow to anger *is* better than the mighty, And he who rules his spirit than he who takes a city." **(Proverbs 16:32 NKJV)** This is the motivation for what Paul says we should do as he writes to the Ephesians. *"Be angry, and do not sin":* do not let the sun go down on your wrath, nor give place to the devil." **(Ephesians 4:26-27 NKJV)** And, he gives our Lord's will for us as he writes to the Colossians. *"But now you yourselves are to put off all these: anger, wrath, malice, blasphemy, filthy language out of your mouth."* **(Colossians 3:8 NKJV)**

Then he further gives us keys to life victory as he enjoins the Philippians to: *"Let* nothing *be done* through selfish ambition or conceit, but in lowliness of mind let each esteem others better than himself." **(Philippians 2:3 NKJV)** and, *"Do all things without complaining and disputing, that you may*

---

[37] William Backus and Marie Chapian. *Telling Yourself the Truth*, 2000, Bethany House Publishers; Minneapolis, MN. P 89.

become blameless and harmless, children of God without fault in the midst of a crooked and perverse generation, among whom you shine as lights in the world."
(Philippians 2:14-15 NKJV)

Do you see the volume of scripture that addresses this issue of fussing? I am more and more convicted. I think I can safely say to you now, since we are a good distance from midpoint in the book, that I am writing this book for myself. You certainly may benefit from it. And, no sooner have I polished this chapter that I fail. Did you hear me? I failed in the very thing I'm writing about. My space was invaded, and I really don't like folks getting deep into my personal space. I voiced my disapproval and the climate changed. I was tired. The other person was tired. We clashed. Now, I have to process that to see if I was at fault. I'll conclude with the verdict!

We have been talking about how fussing is futile. We have seen that fragile lives can engage in fussing - oh so easily. I have tried to give you, the reader, a handle on how the whole world fusses. It is my desire, to give you hope, in the midst of the moral decay, the civil unrest, and the consummation of God's creation. Please hear and read the encouragement to be a victor rather than a victim in this feuding and cantankerous world. You can find strength to overcome fussing in your own life as you read and re-read this book. I hope you will share it with your family and friends. Be strong and lead the way. Be honest with your own feelings and emotions.

> *You can find strength to overcome fussing in your own life.*

While I was serving in the United States Air Force, I belonged to a local Baptist Church. I was teaching Sunday School, trying to sing in the choir and much more. A family was transferred in and joined the same church. The Captain joined the choir as well. I immediately did not like him. He was loud and boisterous and seemed to know "a lot." Too much for my untrained mind! But, he even invited me, a single young airman, over to his house for lunch with his family. I agreed to go. I left feeling more intimidated and really did not grow to like him any better. He was a cocky pilot, I thought. One day a work order came in to our shop. It was an "order" for an electrician to fly over to a nearby base and fix a burned wire and make the plane flyable again. I was given the task.

I grabbed my tool pouch; got on the C-123K and we flew to Duke Field. I repaired the plane so that it could fly. Then, I asked the ground crew, "Who is taking me back?" They said I would have to fly with the plane I "just fixed." Who was the pilot? The very verbal and unlikable Captain! God taught me a huge lesson that day. Be careful who you fuss with and who you choose to NOT like. You may have to put your life in their hands. I did that day.

To fly we must trust! We have to trust the ground crew, the pilot(s); the FAA; the Air Traffic Controllers, and a host of others. So, as we flee from fussing there is much trust involved. We must trust the Holy Spirit residing in us as Christians. We must trust the other party in the fuss to be truthful about their feelings, their emotions, their facts and their promised actions. In the process we need to apply this principle:

"A wrathful man stirs up strife, But he who is slow to anger allays contention" **(Proverbs 15:18 NKJV)**.

195

Although I don't rack up frequent flyer miles, travelling across the nation or around the world is not a problem any longer for me. One must understand the basics of travel and use good protocol to manage any trip that includes flying. Getting free of the habitual fuss is like taking a flight on a jetliner.

> *Triumph over anything is not cheap.*

Here are some simple steps.

1. Know your destination.
2. Know the purpose of your trip.
3. Determine the cost.
4. Follow the Rules.
    a. What will you need to take (pack)?
    b. (And today – what do you NOT take)?
5. Determine who will go with you or do you go alone?
6. Enjoy the trip.
7. Prepare for arrival.

Your destination in reading this book is to find that strength and skill to overcome petty, futile fussing. It is helping others cease and decrease the time they spend in conflict with others. Your purpose in studying the scriptures racked up in

196

Fuss! Fuss! **Fuss!**

this guide is to grow in faith enough to trust God to give you total victory over fussing now in your life and the fussing that's coming that will destroy the world as we know it. We all must pay the price for this kind of victory. Triumph over anything is not cheap. Freedom is not free, as most conservative people know and believe. While we don't ever need to become legalistic, we do need to follow the "rules" and the principles that bring peace in the midst of chaos, light in the midst of darkness, and hope out of despair. So, start UNPACKING and PACKING. Pack into your mind and heart the truth of God. Unpack those destructive emotions and habits that will make you a loser. You don't fly alone on this journey. You have the Holy Spirit to be your Teacher, Comforter and Guide. He will get you there, quickly and safely. You must determine that through this journey, this warfare, this growth spurt; you will enjoy the trip. Refuse to just endure life. Enjoy life! Nehemiah of Bible fame, reminded his people that "the joy of the Lord is [our] strength." **(Nehemiah 8:10)** When you arrive, celebrate. You will find many to share your joy and peace. Contrariwise, you will be alone if you throw a pity party because of the FUSS.

197

It might be wise to contact a travel agency for guidelines, to fly to some place in the world. In like manner, it is wise to follow the guidelines God provides for flying away from conflict and the fussing that ensues. One day while browsing the internet for an illustration for a sermon, akin to this book, I found the following story about freedom and dying to self:

> Let me tell you the true story of a duke, who lived during the fourteenth century, named Raynald III [pronounced Ray- nawl, the third (brackets mine)]. Raynald III lived a life of indulgence and was obese. His Latin nickname was Crassus, which means, "fat."

> One day Raynald and his younger brother, Edward, got into a vicious fight and Edward planned and executed a triumphant revolt against Raynald. Edward took his older brother into custody but did not take his life. Edward decided to construct a room around Raynald in the Nieuwkerk Castle and promised his brother that he would enjoy freedom once again when he was able to leave the room.

> Now for the average Joe this wouldn't have been much of a challenge, because the room Edward built had a number of windows and a door of near-normal size. Neither the door nor the windows were locked - - they weren't barricaded. So, you're getting the picture by now. In order to experience his freedom again Raynald needed to lose weight. But his brother

Edward was no dummy, because he knew just how to keep Raynald imprisoned. Every day he would send Raynald an assortment of tasty foods. And what took place is just sad. Instead of dieting his way to freedom, Raynald grew more overweight and he stayed in that room for ten years until his brother [Edward] died. But by that time his health was so awful that he kicked the bucket within a year.

We can say that Raynald III was a prisoner of his own appetite for food.[38]

Government is like that – not just in the USA, but around the world. Check out the men, and women, leaders in government that seek to fill up their appetites for power. These people are prisoners of their own appetite for power. And, they create fussing and fighting that is futile, rather than leading their nation to prosperity, health and wellness, and a living environment that promotes mature citizens.

The Bible says:

> **"Make no friendship with an angry man, And with a furious man do not go, Lest you learn his ways And set a snare for your soul." (Proverbs 22:24-25 NKJV)**

---

[38] http://www.sermoncentral.com/Illustrations/SearchResults.asp?sscat=illustrations&sitesearch=ros-raynald&rk=raynald&keyword=raynald

One of the most helpful and productive seminars I participated in and received certification for while working on my doctorate was "Peacemaker Ministries." This conflict management course offers very concrete and definite Biblical solutions to offenses caused by fussing and fighting. According to Ken Sande, the first way to avoid conflict is to "overlook" someone's offense, or fault. It is part of the Peacemaking Responses on what he calls "The Slippery Slope."[39]

Perhaps this is exactly what Paul had in mind when he wrote to the Roman church:

> **"If it is possible, as much as depends on you, live peaceably with all men. Beloved, do not avenge yourselves, but *rather* give place to wrath; for it is written, *"Vengeance is Mine, I will repay,"* says the Lord. Therefore *"If your enemy is hungry, feed him; If he is thirsty, give him a drink; For in so doing you will heap coals of fire on his head."* Do not be overcome by evil, but overcome evil with good."**
> **Romans 12:18-21 (NKJV)**

---

[39] Ken Sande, *The Peacemaker*, Baker Books, Grand Rapids, Michigan, 2004. P. 22-23.

And again, the Writer of Proverbs says:

"Where *there is* no wood, the fire goes out; And where *there is* no talebearer, strife ceases." **Proverbs 26:20 (NKJV)** When someone is caught in a "brawl" or a multi-person conflict the wise thing to do is get away from the fuss as quickly as possible. Let's imagine a pastor who has good, qualified leaders in the church where he serves. They plan an activity that includes many people with different functions. He is not in charge but has been invited to the event. The only part he has in the event was given to him two days before everyone gathered. The day of the event the pastor arrives after the activities are under way, to "observe and enjoy" what his members were doing

The real "leader" of the event began to scold him for not being "on time" which was never communicated to him that he should be. He is suddenly placed in a position of failure before the group even though he did not plan nor have a part in planning.

The real clincher in the conflict was when a different leader, the person in charge of the whole event, brought another leader to him and asked for his opinion about conducting the event in a stadium the next year. The pastor quickly replied that the budget could not handle such an event. The church leader was offended. The word spread to other leadership that the pastor simply "cut her off" and was unkind and harsh to her. Later the pastor got word that the leader/member was offended and tried to apologize to her. She would not hear of it. The original event leader got involved and she would not listen either. The pastor felt defeated. The next week a deacon called the pastor to take him to task. Now the pastor is involved in a multi-layered conflict. The deacon began to spread unkind words around about the pastor and the conflict was growing. It seemed no one wanted to hear the pastor's side, as no one came to ask him about his side of the story. The damage had been done. The pastor lost a lot of self-esteem and influence among the members he had so graciously served for years. Time healed the wounds in this case but it could have been much nastier.

If the original party in this clash had simply "overlooked" or at least had done what the Bible says, and confronted one on one, then this would never have gotten out of hand. But, it did get out of hand and the pastor became the bad guy. The members who acted unkindly to their pastor certainly need to learn how to resolve conflict. This story is testimony that sometimes it is impossible to "fly away" from a fuss. When faced with this kind of fuss, one must simply try to resolve the differences, demonstrate a willingness to make things right, and wait for healing to take place.

The Bible says: "He who is of a proud heart stirs up strife, But he who trusts in the LORD will be prospered." **(Proverbs 28:25 NKJV)** and, "An angry man stirs up strife, And a furious man abounds in transgression." **(Proverbs 29:22 NKJV)**

In the Eighties, I worked with the Georgia Baptist Convention as a Discipleship Training consultant. During that time, I was asked to teach a book, *Determining My Values* during one of the Youth Evangelism Conferences. The author, Clyde Lee Herring, shared an illustration about the conscience. "A little girl seemed puzzled. She asked her mother one day, "Mother, what is a conscience?" Her mother replied, "A conscience is the little voice inside that tells you when you're doing wrong." That night the little girl knelt by her bed for prayer. She prayed for lots of things and thanked God for her blessings of the day. Then she finished her prayer, "Oh, God, please make that little voice loud."[40]

---

[40] Clyde Lee Herring. *Determining My Values.* Convention Press. Nashville 1979, p. 22.

We all need to hear that little voice of the Spirit of God as we engage in a fuss. We ought to hear Him saying some of the things we have learned from Scripture. In that way we can "overlook" and we can negotiate our way through the fuss and avoid being entangled in Satan's web.

Patricia and I watched a movie some time ago entitled, "Princess Diaries"[41] a 2001 Disney movie, which starred Julie Andrews (Queen Clarisse Rinaldi) and Anne Hathaway (princess Mia Thermopolis). In the movie there is a scene where Mia is involved in a wreck with a trolley. To diffuse the fuss over the accident, Queen Clarisse uses some kind words and positive affirmation with the trolley workers. As Patricia and I watched this scene we saw the power of this technique in resolving the problem. We dubbed this the "Genovia effect."

Although we give it a worldly name, it is simply a Biblical admonition of kindness and dying to self. We have since been in some similar situations and remind each other that

---

[41]

http://www.bing.com/movies/search/synopsis?q=The+Princess+Diaries&id=2343c011-28d2-4406-b4fa-dd9eae20fb13&where=Atlanta%2c+GA&latlon=33.800972%7e-84.388535&FORM=DTPSHA

we need to use the "Genovia effect." Maybe, just maybe we can get the message across, that to avoid fussing we must simply start employing it more often!

And, personally, I still need to polish that tool for use every day! The Bible affirms such a decision:

> "Finally, all *of you be* of one mind, having compassion for one another; love as brothers, *be* tenderhearted, *be* courteous;
> not returning evil for evil or reviling for reviling, but on the contrary blessing, knowing that you were called to this, that you may inherit a blessing.
> For *"He who would love life And see good days, Let him refrain his tongue from evil, And his lips from speaking deceit.*
> *Let him turn away from evil and do good; Let him seek peace and pursue it.*
> *For the eyes of the LORD are on the righteous, And His ears are open to their prayers; But the face of the LORD is against those who do evil."*
> And who *is* he who will harm you if you become followers of what is good?
> But even if you should suffer for righteousness' sake, *you are* blessed. *"And do not be afraid of their threats, nor be troubled."*
> But sanctify the Lord God in your hearts, and always *be* ready to *give* a defense to everyone who asks you a reason for the hope that is in you, with meekness and fear;
> having a good conscience, that when they defame you as evildoers, those who revile your good conduct in Christ may be ashamed.

> **For *it is* better, if it is the will of God, to suffer for doing good than for doing evil."**
> **1 Peter 3:8-17 (NKJV)**

Anger can be a stronghold! We must do spiritual warfare. Living a life of anger will render a person useless and unproductive.   There are better ways to handle life's problems than being angry all the time. If you are constantly angry it is a red flag telling you that there is danger in your life, caused not by someone else, but brought about by your own spiritual condition.

> **"You have heard that it was said, *'An eye for an eye and a tooth for a tooth.'***
> **But I tell you not to resist an evil person. But whoever slaps you on your right cheek, turn the other to him also.**
> **If anyone wants to sue you and take away your tunic, let him have *your* cloak also.**
> **And whoever compels you to go one mile, go with him two.**
> **Give to him who asks you, and from him who wants to borrow from you do not turn away.**
> **You have heard that it was said, *'You shall love your neighbor* and hate your enemy.'**
>
> **But I say to you, love your enemies, bless those who curse you, do good to those who hate you, and pray for those who spitefully use you and persecute you,**
> **that you may be sons of your Father in heaven; for He makes His sun rise on the evil and on the**

good, and sends rain on the just and on the unjust.
For if you love those who love you, what reward have you? Do not even the tax collectors do the same?

And if you greet your brethren only, what do you do more *than others?* Do not even the tax collectors do so?
Therefore you shall be perfect, just as your Father in heaven is perfect." Matthew 5:38-48 (NKJV)

"But I say to you who hear: Love your enemies, do good to those who hate you,
bless those who curse you, and pray for those who spitefully use you." Luke 6:27-28 (NKJV)

The challenge of dying to self and knowing when to stand.

Fuss! Fuss! Fuss!

Chapter 12

Standing as You Flee

STANDING: what it means.

When I use the term "to stand" or "stand firm" I am mirroring the Apostle Paul as he wrote to the Ephesians about spiritual warfare. He said in essence, when the battle is over let it be known by all concerned and all involved in the conflict that you finished by "standing" – or you were "left standing." (Which is a positive thing!) This means that you were not defeated. It means that you did not give up ground. You did not surrender. You were victorious!

Standing has to do with what one believes and being willing to take a position or give a defense for it. Peter reminds us that we need to defend our faith:

> **"But sanctify the Lord God in your hearts, and always be ready to give a defense to everyone who asks you a reason for the hope that is in you, with meekness and fear; (1 Peter 3:15 NKJV)**

The word "defense" is a translation of the Greek "apologia" or making an apology for the position you take. It does NOT mean apologizing for what you say or do when you stand for what you believe. It means that you can give a rational logic, and factual explanation for your belief and action.

Jesus in teaching His disciples, gives all believers assurance that nothing will prevail against His church. Matthew records the conversation:

> **When Jesus came into the region of Caesarea Philippi, He asked His disciples, saying, "Who do men say that I, the Son of Man, am?" So they said, "Some say John the Baptist, some Elijah, and others Jeremiah or one of the prophets." He said to them, "But who do you say that I am?" Simon Peter answered and said, "You are the Christ, the Son of the living God." Jesus answered and said to him, "Blessed are you, Simon Bar-Jonah, for flesh and blood has not revealed this to you, but My Father who is in heaven. And I also say to you that you are Peter, and on this rock I**

> **will build My church, and the gates of Hades shall**
> **not prevail against it. And I will give you the keys**
> **of the kingdom of heaven, and whatever you bind**
> **on earth will be bound in heaven, and whatever**
> **you loose on earth will be loosed in heaven."**
> **Matthew 16:13-19 NKJV)**

Now notice, Jesus clearly tells his disciples that as time moves forward, it will be paramount for the church to be militant. When He said that the gates of Hades (or Hell) will not prevail, it implies that the church is attacking the gates and will bash those gates down and win the victory over Satan and his evil dominion. Oh, if the church could just grasp that today! If the church embraced that idea we would see cleaner communities, less crime, less brutality, less abuse, less murder and the like. Homes would be stronger. Businesses would be trustworthy. Healthcare would be classic and we would not be suffering from socialism. Why? Because we would be attacking Hollywood, the media, anti-American groups that are destroying the foundations of home, business, and our form of government in America. What would our world be like if the Church fully embraced this scripture?

And in that same context, Jesus gives the solution to conflict within the Church:

> "Moreover if your brother sins against you, go and tell him his fault between you and him alone. If he hears you, you have gained your brother.
> But if he will not hear, take with you one or two more, that 'by the mouth of two or three witnesses every word may be established.'
> And if he refuses to hear them, tell it to the church. But if he refuses even to hear the church, let him be to you like a heathen and a tax collector. Assuredly, I say to you, whatever you bind on earth will be bound in heaven, and whatever you loose on earth will be loosed in heaven.
> Again I say to you that if two of you agree on earth concerning anything that they ask, it will be done for them by My Father in heaven.
> For where two or three are gathered together in My name, I am there in the midst of them."
> **(Matthew 18:15-20 NKJV)**

Please note how Christians today misuse part of this scripture. When we say that our prayer meetings are based on "where two or three are gathered together and Christ is in the midst of us" we err. In context, Christ was saying that He would be in the midst of those who are trying to resolve conflict, whether it is two or three or more.

In my own ministry experience I have seen individual believers, who are engaged in conflict, use very unbiblical actions to try to solve the fuss. And, that, too often! Standing in the midst of conflict requires discipleship, peacemaking and wisdom. Why do Christians, of all people, not practice Matthew 5 and Matthew 18? Maybe people just won't take the time. Maybe they are afraid to get involved. Maybe no one has taught them the Biblical truth.

Conflict is not easily taught. One of the better books on dealing with conflict in a positive way is John Trent, Rodney Cox and Eric Tooker's *Leading From Your Strengths*.[42] These authors "offer a process for building close-knit ministry teams."[43] Throughout the book the reader learns about his/her own personality and how to relate to other personalities. Understanding "personality" is the key to avoiding conflict and when conflict happens to resolve it in a positive, productive way.

Again, Paul would have every Christian soldier "stand" and not fall, STAND and not allow the Devil to defeat them or win over their mission. Now let me unpack Ephesians six so that you might gain the practical help it provides.

---

[42] John Trent, Rodney Cox, Eric Tooker, Leading from Your Strengths, Broadman & Holman: Nashville, TN., 2004

[43] Ibid, p. 99.

The passage that deals with conflict actually begins back in chapter five of Ephesians. Paul addresses the different relationships a follower of Christ might possess. He begins with wives and moves through the list of roles – husbands, children, fathers, masters, bondservants. Then he addresses everyone as "brothers." As we read from Ephesians six, the Apostle lays out the plan for the Christian to be successful in conflict.

> **10 Finally, my brethren, be strong in the Lord and in the power of His might.**
> **11 Put on the whole armor of God, that you may be able to stand against the wiles of the devil.**
> **12 For we do not wrestle against flesh and blood, but against principalities, against powers, against the rulers of the darkness of this age, against spiritual hosts of wickedness in the heavenly places.**
> **13 Therefore take up the whole armor of God, that you may be able to withstand in the evil day, and having done all, to stand.**
> **14 Stand therefore, having girded your waist with truth, having put on the breastplate of righteousness,**
> **15 and having shod your feet with the preparation of the gospel of peace;**
> **16 above all, taking the shield of faith with which you will be able to quench all the fiery darts of the wicked one.**
> **17 And take the helmet of salvation, and the sword of the Spirit, which is the word of God;**
> **18 praying always with all prayer and supplication in the Spirit, being watchful to this**

**end with all perseverance and supplication for
all the saints-- (Ephesians 6:10-18 NKJV)**

To win over fussing, we must begin deliberately each day to
"put on the whole armor of God" and then be aware of the
armor throughout the day. Let's look at it closely.

Here's how I do it. I wake up and realize that I am into a
new day. As I turn to place my feet on the floor, before I
stand up, I pray asking the Father to give me the armor.
Prayer is the key to getting the armor placed on the person.
So, I thank God that I have the Helmet of Salvation. That is
given to us when we receive Christ as Lord. The helmet
protects the brain, the mind. Our mind is the battle ground
for conflict. We must first conquer our thought life. Bring
every thought under His control. Then, I thank God for the
Breastplate of Righteousness. That was given to me at
salvation. I have no righteousness in myself. But I claim the
righteousness of Christ as a believer in order that I may
approach the Father. Christ is our righteousness. In Him
alone we are permitted to stand before the throne of God,
dressed in His righteousness, free from condemnation, and
considered a son.

Next, I ask God to help me wear the "girdle" of truth. It is the belt placed around the waist. Truth should be our appetite in all that we do. We get truth by ingesting daily the Word of God. I should always speak the truth or there will be conflict. Sometimes that requires dying to self. I should always protect the truth, and promote the truth. Sometimes that requires standing. Then, with the truth I need to wear the sandals of peace. If I speak the truth then I must do so in love which makes for peace. There are times that the truth hurts. But, the one, who is affected adversely by the truth, either about themselves, or someone or something needs to know that truth is shared out of love. What is truth? It is always in line with God's Word.

Next, I take the shield of faith, realizing that wherever I go, whatever I do "today" will have to be done in faith. That faith protects me against the methods the devil might use against me. Finally, I take the only offensive part of the armor – the Sword of the Spirit, which is the Bible, God's Holy Word. Remember we have "ingested the Word." We must also: remember the Word, meditate on the Word and apply the Word. With the armor on, I now stand up and face the day ready to "stand" against the Evil One.

One of the best books that ministered to me during a period of church conflict several years ago, (turned into days) was ***Six Sure Ways to Solve Any Problem No Matter What*** by Dr. Wayne Diehm. The imagery in Dr. Diehm's book stuck with me. He introduces his message with a story about a bee that was in his house. He could not get the bee to go out an open door no matter how hard he tried. The bee kept pounding against the windows trying to get out, till it died, when just inches away it could be free.

WE get locked into conflict and WON'T get out because we will not use the open window or door to do so. God has provided the open doors and windows to set us free. Dr. Diehm offers the "windows" we try to use to get out of our troubles and conflicts. Here is his list of windows which will not work.

1. Ignoring the problem
2. Protecting ourselves from the problem
3. Retreating from the problem
4. Blaming (someone else or something)
5. Negative Transfer (converting to a disorder of health; becoming negative about everything; or going to opposite extremes)

6. Positive Transfer (turn our attention to another

direction)

Then he gives us a list of "doors" that work, avenues "open"

to us by which we can be set free.

1. Defining (understand and define exactly what
you are faced with)
2. Opting (determine all options and decide on the
best one to use)
3. Organizing (deciding on steps to take and
resources needed)
4. Learning (through trying out the optional path)
5. Persevering (stay the course till the victory is
won)
6. Motivating (using emotions, knowledge and
behavior)

I highly suggest that you use this book (digest it) to get a

handle on conquering fussing in your relationships. Since

most of us are not going to use "much" or "very little"

psychology to resolve conflict, let me suggest that we use the

Bible along with the understanding gleaned from Diem's

book. So how do you do Spiritual Warfare? It can be

explained as simply as this: Use the Word of God. That is

what Jesus did when tempted by Satan.

Harold Lindsell wrote *The World the Flesh & the Devil* while he was editor – publisher of "Christianity Today." He says:

> "The Christian life is a continual spiritual warfare, part of God's plan of the ages which does not end until death (1 Timothy 6:12). There is every reason to approach it with fear and trembling, but there is no reason to run away from it.
> . . . In the midst of tribulation God makes visible his delivering power and brings the believer to a place of fuller and deeper trust in him."[44]

In one of my pastorates, I saw a young man who had pretty much messed up his life with uncontrolled passions and taste for liquor and drugs. He started attending church again with his parents. One Sunday, he moved forward in the invitation and rededicated his life. On a follow-up visit he asked me to teach him to die to self. Wow! That was a pastor's dream. Would that all our members had such a desire! I

> **He asked me to teach him to die to self.**

[44] Harold Lindsell, *The World, The Flesh &The Devil;* World Wide Publications 1313 Hennepin Avenue, Minneapolis, MN 55403, 1973, p. 39.

did the best I could for a short period of time. But we moved and I lost contact with him.

Today, I certainly would have told him one of the best ways to do that is to learn all the "one another's" of the New Testament. Dr. Don McMinn, author of *Love One Another*, does an amazing job with that book. In it he teaches how to apply these "one another" passages.[45] For instance, when we practice preferring one another we actually are "standing for the faith" in the sense that we are practicing selfless love, and we are dying to self in that we are overcoming the desire to be first. Therefore, dying to self is standing for the faith.

Part of owning the fuss and resolving conflict in our life is to understand our personality and the way the other person is wired. When we recognize the personality traits in a fuss then we can better handle the dialog, the emotions, the body language and all that is involved.

Putting distance from the fuss does not mean that you and I ignore it, or pretend that it is not there, or that it is someone's else's responsibility. To put distance between you and the

---

[45] Don McMinn, *Love One Another : 20 Practical Lessons,* iPlace Press,

conflict does not mean putting distance between you and the other person. That only prolongs the conflict and sets both of you up later for a bigger explosion. It does mean that you do what a herd of little Texas donkeys do when they have conflict with wolves or some other threatening animal. They get in a circle, put their heads together and turn their backsides to the enemy. That way, when the attacking animal approaches, they kick the ever-living stew out of it.

We need to always identify the problem in a fuss and attack the problem not the person. We ought to attempt putting our heads together, turn our kickers to the enemy and protect our relationships and one another. Sometimes, however, when all has been attempted and the other person in a fuss will not be reasonable, then distance from that person is inevitable, except for divine intervention.

When we talk about flight from fussing, we are getting distance from the fuss. God is our Helper. The Word of God has power to free us. We have to discipline ourselves to respond to people and things in such a way that we do not stay in the fuss. Isaiah of Old Testament fame declared:

> **"Fear not, for I *am* with you; Be not dismayed, for I *am* your God. I will strengthen you, Yes, I**

will help you, I will uphold you with My
righteous right hand.'
"Behold, all those who were incensed against you
Shall be ashamed and disgraced; They shall be
as nothing, And those who strive with you shall
perish. You shall seek them and not find them--
Those who contended with you. Those who war
against you Shall be as nothing, As a nonexistent
thing." (Isaiah 41:10-12 NKJV)

Matthew the Gospel writer says:

"Moreover if your brother sins against you, go
and tell him his fault between you and him alone.
If he hears you, you have gained your brother.
But if he will not hear, take with you one or two
more, that *'by the mouth of two or three witnesses
every word may be established.'*

And if he refuses to hear them, tell *it* to the
church. But if he refuses even to hear the church,
let him be to you like a heathen and a tax
collector." (Matthew 18:15-17 NKJV)

Paul writes:

"Receive one who is weak in the faith, *but* not to
disputes over doubtful things." (Romans 14:1
NKJV) "Therefore let us pursue the things
which make for peace and the things by which
one may edify another." (Romans 14:19 NKJV)
"Now I urge you, brethren, note those who cause
divisions and offenses, contrary to the doctrine
which you learned, and avoid them. For those

> who are such do not serve our Lord Jesus Christ,
> but their own belly, and by smooth words and
> flattering speech deceive the hearts of the
> simple." (Romans 16:17-18 NKJV)

In order for us to put distance between ourselves and a fuss,

we can use Michael Zigarelli's posted article entitled "Eight

Ways to Improve Your People Skills"[46] which are:

1. *Don't complain*
2. *Smile*
3. *Listen closely and actively*
4. *Praise others*
5. *Show gratitude*
6. *Talk about others' interests*
7. *Remember names*
8. *Make a sacrifice*

The challenge of dying to self and knowing when to stand.

---

[46] http://www.lifeway.com/Article/Ways-to-improve-your-people-skills (note: Michael Zigarelli is professor of Leadership and Strategy at Messiah College, Mechanicsburg, Pennsylvania, and the former Dean of the Regent University School of Business.)

Fuss! Fuss! Fuss!

Chapter 13

Forgiveness for the Fuss

A man was recently released from prison, having served twenty-five (25) years. He was proven innocent of the crime for which he had been incarcerated. The evidence that released him was a piece of paper placed in his legal FILE, which was there all the time. The document proved he was at Disney World with his kids when the crime happened.[47] In like manner the answer to the release from sin's power and the salvation and redemption that we all seek, is right there in the WORD of God all the time. We just need to be faithful to use it.

---

[47] http://www.businessinsider.com/innocent-guy-released-from-prison-25-years-after-prosecutors-suppressed-disney-world-rece-2014-4

I need forgiveness, almost daily. All sin needs forgiving. It is not automatic. Our fusses are not forgiven automatically either. Forgiveness is an act of grace. Those who learn how to forgive are champions. Those who refuse to forgive are victims. Forgiveness is a power essential to healthy living. What does forgiveness mean? Most fussing is sin. Some fussing is righteous. Unrighteous fussing is worthless and we ought to pray with the Psalmist that God would show us what is worthless.

One of the ways to curb fussing in a family (it could be used in the workplace as well) is to have family devotions. If the family would gather together and read 1 Corinthians 13 every day for 30 days it will make a huge difference in attitudes and actions.

Jesus fussed. The Christ had conflict with the Scribes and other religious groups known as the Pharisees and Sadducees. They tried to trap him in His words with the intent to not only silence Him but eventually have Him killed.

> [18] Then *some* Sadducees, who say there is no resurrection, came to Him; and they asked Him, saying:
> [19] "Teacher, Moses wrote to us that if a man's brother dies, and leaves *his* wife behind, and

leaves no children, his brother should take his wife and raise up offspring for his brother.

20 Now there were seven brothers. The first took a wife; and dying, he left no offspring.

21 And the second took her, and he died; nor did he leave any offspring. And the third likewise.

22 So the seven had her and left no offspring. Last of all the woman died also.

23 Therefore, in the resurrection, when they rise, whose wife will she be? For all seven had her as wife."

24 Jesus answered and said to them, "Are you not therefore mistaken, because you do not know the Scriptures nor the power of God?

25 For when they rise from the dead, they neither marry nor are given in marriage, but are like angels in heaven.

26 But concerning the dead, that they rise, have you not read in the book of Moses, in the *burning bush passage,* how God spoke to him, saying, *'I am the God of Abraham, the God of Isaac, and the God of Jacob'?*

27 He is not the God of the dead, but the God of the living. You are therefore greatly mistaken."

28 Then one of the scribes came, and having heard them reasoning together, perceiving that He had answered them well, asked Him, "Which is the first commandment of all?"

29 Jesus answered him, "The first of all the commandments *is: 'Hear, O Israel, the LORD our God, the LORD is one.*

30 *And you shall love the LORD your God with all your heart, with all your soul, with all your mind, and with all your strength.'* This *is* the first commandment.

31 And the second, like *it, is* this: *'You shall love*

your neighbor as yourself.' There is no other commandment greater than these."
³² So the scribe said to Him, "Well *said,* Teacher. You have spoken the truth, for there is one God, and there is no other but He.
³³ And to love Him with all the heart, with all the understanding, with all the soul, and with all the strength, and to love one's neighbor as oneself, is more than all the whole burnt offerings and sacrifices."
³⁴ Now when Jesus saw that he answered wisely, He said to him, "You are not far from the kingdom of God." But after that no one dared question Him.   (Mark 12:18-34 NKJV)

Jesus fussed with esteemed leaders of Judaism over their loyalty to God the Father. He told them they were not committed to the God of Abraham, Isaac and Jacob, but of the Devil, the Father of lies. He tells His disciples about His imminent departure from Earth. The Jewish leaders overhear this and pick a fuss with Jesus.

²¹ Then Jesus said to them again, "I am going away, and you will seek Me, and will die in your sin. Where I go you cannot come."
²² So the Jews said, "Will He kill Himself, because He says, 'Where I go you cannot come'?"
²³ And He said to them, "You are from beneath; I am from above. You are of this world; I am not of this world.
²⁴ Therefore I said to you that you will die in your sins; for if you do not believe that I am *He,*

228

you will die in your sins."
25 Then they said to Him, "Who are You?" And
Jesus said to them, "Just what I have been
saying to you from the beginning.
26 I have many things to say and to judge
concerning you, but He who sent Me is true; and
I speak to the world those things which I heard
from Him."
27 They did not understand that He spoke to
them of the Father.   (John 8:21-27 NKJV)

Jesus committed no sin. Thus, fussing is not always sinful.

Paul fussed. Paul was a sinner. He was also a man full of grace. But there were times he was embroiled in a fuss but committed no sin in doing so. He was on a mission. In fact, Paul the Apostle took at least three major mission journeys. On all three journeys he encountered people who were conflictive.   Paul admonished his readers out a life of personal experience and a calling by Christ to forgive. Can you imagine the Apostle Paul NOT forgiving all those who hurt him?

Peter fussed. Peter even fussed with the Lord. It was over the matter of "washing feet." He fussed with others. I have (along with most pastors) fussed with congregations. I won some. I lost some. Sometimes the fuss helped. Most of the time it hurt – me, them or both of us.

229

Forgiveness is not just a topic for a preacher's sermon. It is not just an admonition by someone who thinks they know how you feel and are trying to solve YOUR problems. It is not a platitude that only sounds good. It is not a weakness to avoid.

> *If we confess our sins, He is faithful and just to forgive us our sins and to cleanse us from all unrighteousness.*
> *(1 John 1:9 (NKJV)*

1. What it is

It is release. We release the other person from the injury, the offense, the sin committed against us or our loved ones. It is sometimes a process by which we must work to get to the rim of a devastating emotional gorge.

2. How it works

Just like Jesus, we have the attitude that we want the Father to forgive them because we are willing to love them enough to let the offense, sin or injury go. That is an action born out of a grateful heart because we ourselves have been forgiven. Jesus preached love your enemies. Then He proved it, demonstrated it by dying on a cross and said, "Father, forgive them, for they do not know what they are doing." We prove that we have forgiven others by not bringing up

230

the conflict again. We don't keep a "crime against me" list.
Love is not easily provoked by previous wrong doings.
(Wow! We need to work on that one before someone is
written off, don't we?) Here is the bottom line: LOVE. We
do not really love someone unless we have forgiven them.
Forgive like God forgives so that you are empowered to love
like God loves. When we forgive it is an act of love, thus we
are being obedient to God's command to love one another
and love our enemies.

Jesus taught His disciples:

> **21 Then Peter came to Him and said, "Lord,
> how often shall my brother sin against me, and I
> forgive him? Up to seven times?"**
> **22 Jesus said to him, "I do not say to you, up to
> seven times, but up to seventy times seven.**
> **23 Therefore the kingdom of heaven is like a
> certain king who wanted to settle accounts with
> his servants.**
> **24 And when he had begun to settle accounts,
> one was brought to him who owed him ten
> thousand talents.**
> **25 But as he was not able to pay, his master
> commanded that he be sold, with his wife and
> children and all that he had, and that payment
> be made.**
> **26 The servant therefore fell down before him,
> saying, 'Master, have patience with me, and I
> will pay you all.'**
> **27 Then the master of that servant was moved
> with compassion, released him, and forgave him
> the debt.**

28 But that servant went out and found one of his fellow servants who owed him a hundred denarii; and he laid hands on him and took him by the throat, saying, 'Pay me what you owe!'
29 So his fellow servant fell down at his feet and begged him, saying, 'Have patience with me, and I will pay you all.'
30 And he would not, but went and threw him into prison till he should pay the debt.
31 So when his fellow servants saw what had been done, they were very grieved, and came and told their master all that had been done.
32 Then his master, after he had called him, said to him, 'You wicked servant! I forgave you all that debt because you begged me.
33 Should you not also have had compassion on your fellow servant, just as I had pity on you?'
34 And his master was angry, and delivered him to the torturers until he should pay all that was due to him.
35 So My heavenly Father also will do to you if each of you, from his heart, does not forgive his brother his trespasses." (Matthew 18:21-35 (NKJV)

3. When it's done

The sooner the better, for the sake of your own health and the health of those you love and influence. We ought to take care of the need to give forgiveness immediately and the need to ask for forgiveness on the same day of the offense. By doing so we assure ourselves that we are demonstrating maturity, and will be known as a peacemaker.

4. Who it involves

Forgiveness involves the perpetrator, the injured and God.

We either gain a friend when we forgive or <u>we at least remove ourselves from the toxic relationship</u> that is enthralled in a futile, frantic fuss. Many times, in Christian work I had to forgive someone. It may have been someone who lied about me. Someone may have manipulated a committee meeting and undermined my family's welfare by reducing my salary. It certainly was a time when someone pulled a gun on me and was willing to kill me for something I said or did.

5. Benefits of forgiveness – lose the baggage; gain freedom

We are not chained to injury, incidents, inconveniences, and inflaming words by other people. Freedom rules!

How is the fuss wrapped? That is: what kind of personality does a fuss have. The answer is simple. It depends on the person doing the fussing. Sometimes it comes in a nicely wrapped box. Sometimes in a bucket with a bow on top. Sometimes in a small envelope. Sometimes in a rough, rugged old box. When emotion is attached; and it always is, then we have to deal with those emotions, using our spiritual, mental and physical abilities. But, where there is greed, avarice, bitterness, etc., there is sin in the fuss. That is where forgiveness must get dynamic, directed and deliberate. Dr. Luke who wrote both the Gospel which bears his name and the book of Acts in the New Testament, tells us: God has the power **"to open their eyes, in order to turn them from darkness to light, and from the power of Satan to God, that they may receive forgiveness of sins and an inheritance among those who are sanctified by faith in Me (Acts 26:18 NKJV).** The very dynamic of identifying what a fuss is about, and what the personality and condition of a person is, will create an atmosphere whereby God can open eyes and turn them from the darkness of sin to the light of his grace and love. Forgiveness is the potential result. Relationships can be salvaged and changed. The Gospel can be presented and God will be glorified!

The challenge of dying to self and knowing when to stand.

Chapter 14

Dying to Self in order to Forgive

Unresolved conflict (fussing) is like hang nails. They catch on every movement of our conscience until the problem is resolved. Sometimes conflict can be resolved by a simple act of forgiveness. Let me illustrate the power available to you for overcoming fussing by using what's called "The VIN diagram. We will place three words in three circles: FACTS, FUSS, and FORGIVE. These three essentials are linked together and must be engaged by you and me to resolve conflict and gain victory.

> *It is imperative to determine what is in our heart if we are going to resolve any conflict!*

Facts: Face them. Facts are true. Jesus said the truth will set us free. We are free to respond to the fuss when we have the facts together. We can make rational, wise decisions when we know the truth. Change can take place based on facts. The consequences of our decisions will be apparent. Where there is a need for repentance on our part, we can humbly take steps in that direction. Or, if no repentance is needed, we can stand our ground. If you will simply enter the circle or bring someone else into the circle of facts, forgiveness is close by.

Fuss: There is more to a fuss than facts. Humans are created to have a value system and that drives our emotions. The

236

values we hold may be in line with the culture, or our values could be based on something counter culture. Conflict results when two systems cannot cooperate or coexist. It is imperative to determine what is in our heart if we are going to resolve any conflict. Figure out the real problem. When we identify the facts and understand the parties in the fuss, we can state clearly and completely what the fuss is about. We have to name, realistically all the people involved.

Forgiveness: In order for us to experience Biblical forgiveness we must use the Word of God. Some person will say, "I can forgive but I will NEVER forget!" This implies that true forgiveness is not

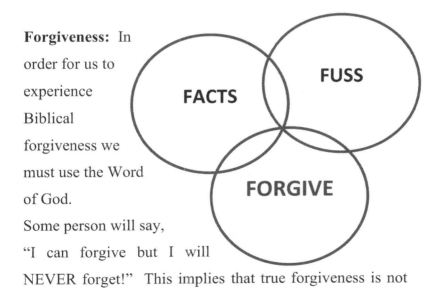

being done. The hurt and pain we experience in a fuss will always, always leave a scar on us and in our relationships. True forgiveness does not mean we "forget" the incident; no more than we can say we will NOT have a scar after some physical injury. The scar reminds us of the fuss. It reminds us to behave differently, and/or respond differently. We must get the Mind of Christ around this and let the Mind of Christ rule our attitudes and actions. The Word of God gives faith to forgive. Faith increases the more we hear the Word. We gain strength in our relationships the more we apply the Word. The more we receive the Word of God the more we are filled with the Spirit of God. Then, the fruit of the Spirit is produced in and through us – such things as love, joy, peace, goodness, patience, self-control.   That in turn develops character. Character produces maturity. I believe it was Dwight L. Moody that demonstrated this power by asking a group one day, "How can I get the air out of the glass I hold in my hand?" One person suggested that he use a pump to suck the air out. To that the great evangelist, replied, "That would create a great vacuum and the glass would shatter!"   Other suggestions were offered.   Mr. Moody simply picked up a pitcher of water and filled the glass. Moody commented that the air is all out of the glass and made the point that the Christian does not come to victory by slavishly working at getting rid of evil thoughts and habits, but rather by allowing the Holy Spirit to take control of one's life. That is what Paul meant in Ephesians 5:18 when he told the church not to be drunk with wine, but be "filled" with the Spirit.

One must have all three of these circles working together, overlapping, interacting, moving by God's grace in order to exercise forgiveness Biblically, fully and victoriously. Use the Facts to understand the Fuss and then Forgive.

We need to place the following weapons in our arsenal to defeat ungodly and unprofitable fussing:

**25 Therefore, putting away lying, "Let each one of you speak truth with his neighbor," for we are members of one another.
26 "Be angry, and do not sin": do not let the sun go down on your wrath,
27 nor give place to the devil.
28 Let him who stole steal no longer, but rather let him labor, working with his hands what is good, that he may have something to give him who has need.
29 Let no corrupt word proceed out of your mouth, but what is good for necessary edification, that it may impart grace to the hearers.
30 And do not grieve the Holy Spirit of God, by whom you were sealed for the day of redemption.**

31 Let all bitterness, wrath, anger, clamor, and evil speaking be put away from you, with all malice.
32 And be kind to one another, tenderhearted, forgiving one another, just as God in Christ forgave you. (Ephesians 4:25-32 NKJV).

9 But avoid foolish disputes, genealogies, contentions, and strivings about the law; for they are unprofitable and useless.
10 Reject a divisive man after the first and second admonition, knowing that such a person is warped and sinning, being self-condemned. (Titus 3:9-11 NKJV)

What we are concerned about and what I am sharing with you is called the ministry of reconciliation. The whole book of 2 Corinthians is like a manual on doing or implementing reconciliation. We are living in a broken world. And, if we are honest with God, ourselves and our families, we will admit that we have broken relationships. These relationships can be mended by the Great Physician if we simply go to Him and ask Him to heal us. He will use His Word and His Spirit and His People to make that happen. Will you be open and obedient to that call for reconciliation today?

To be reconciled means to be restored; to be made new again; to begin anew with someone who has been offended by you or who offended you. First and foremost, we need to be reconciled to God. That is absolutely possible. Then, He will empower you to experience reconciliation and wholeness and health in life with others by engaging them in the Gospel and in Body Life (family of God; kingdom of God) truth.

This passage is more easily put into practice with strangers or mere acquaintances than it is with coworkers and family members. In non-family relationships we can diligently avoid disputes that are foolish, and steer away from discussions about non-essentials, remove ourselves from contentious spirits and refuse to be entangled with religious and theological fussing. We can easily reject that divisive person who keeps showing up in our life, especially after we have "admonished" or encouraged that one to be and speak differently. But, a family member, especially one who is close to us is a different matter. This kind of victory calls for some special work. We might have to learn how to change the subject, move the conversation elsewhere, or use the simple method of excusing ourselves. The important thing is for you to put space between the person you are fussing with and yourself. The one thing we need to learn is FORGIVENESS.

Let me add an acrostic to your tools for forgiveness and getting distance from a fuss.

Let's use the word: STAR

1. **S** – Help your opponent be aware of **SELF**.
Open your heart so that will see the real you. Know who you are. Know your weaknesses and strengths. Know your personality.

2. **T** – **TAKE** the initiative to be Responsible.
When a person learns responsibility then that person is ready to grow, mature and achieve God's will in life. Let the other person see you taking responsibility.

3. **A** – You must be aware of **AUTHORITY.**
Learn to submit to the authority in the home; in the school; in government and beyond. Only when man's authority is in violation to God's authority are we free to disobey.

4. **R** – **REWARDS**
When the first three are achieved, then a person can enjoy the **rewards** of a fruitful and effective life.
These four things must be brought to the table when reconciling and solving issues of life plagued by hateful and immature fussing.

Reconciliation is that action we take during and after a fuss to realize joy in life. God desires us to be reconciled to Him and with our fellow human beings. Here are some short steps you can take to be reconciled with your family member, neighbor, co-worker and even strangers in the marketplace.

1. Acknowledge that you have ownership in any controversy.
2. Examine your heart to see if you have responsibility for making the division happen.
3. Go to the individual and seek peace – you may have to approach this as if you offended the person.
4. Avoid being defensive and certainly refuse to blame the one for the event.
5. Ask for forgiveness from the individual (do not say "I'm sorry!" They may agree with you.) ASK: "Will you forgive me?"
6. Be ready to make any restitution you ought to make.
7. Rest in the assurance that you have obeyed God and initiated reconciliation.
8. Move forward in . . .

. . . The challenge of dying to self and knowing when to stand.

Conclusion

Back on page 183 I said that I had failed in one of my encounters with another person. I have processed the matter. Did I fail? Of course, I did. That's because I am a human being. You know what? During the course of writing this book I have failed at fussing MANY TIMES. Ouch! Whoa!

We all will continue to "fail" in a sense till we either die or go to Heaven. I think I would rather use the term "stumbled again." We really do not FAIL unless we choose to not get back UP and start afresh with a situation, a person, a challenge. We can choose to keep learning in the fussing process. The jetliner you ride on to take you across the world, keeps right on "fussing" with air currents, gravity and temperatures. Through applying the laws of aerodynamics and using the specific engineering put into the airplane and all its components, the pilot gets us to our destiny safe and sound (usually). In the same way, God our Creator (our chief Engineer, Pilot, our All in All) keeps us moving along our path in life. The analogy breaks down in the sense that the plane cannot decide to cooperate with the pilot; but we can decide to cooperate with God and keep learning, growing, maturing, and getting better at dying to self and taking the right stands. So, if I just ignore the things I do wrong and do not ask forgiveness from God and those that I hurt or wrong in some way, I become calloused and useless. But, through forgiveness and keeping the relationship clean, we can move forward and mature.

I have used much Scripture in this volume. I hope these verses have spoken to you and given you the insight you need to conquer fussing and feuding in your relationships. Here is one more: **"Bear each other's burdens." (Galatians 6:2 and Galatians 6:5 – both paraphrased) which says basically, "Each person should bear his own load."** There is nothing contradictory in these verses. Nor, is there in the whole of the Bible. A study of the words "burden" and "load" used in these passages, reveal that Paul meant that we should bear those things that we can handle individually on our own. Whereas, some of the problems and difficulties of life are too much for us to "bear" alone and we need help, therefore he uses a different word which is translated here "burdens" or the bigger burden. If we are constantly fussing with someone and we hate it, because it is sin, then we need help bear the burden. It might be another family member, a friend, a pastor, a coworker, a professional counsellor. The truth is, unless we get some help we will continue to be controlled by the fuss and fussing will destroy our relationships and our lives. Again, the truth is, a family, a business, a nation needs help in removing from its system the toxicity of fussing.

In this revision of FUSS! FUSS! FUSS! I have come to believe that fussing will always be with us. But, we don't have to victims in the fuss. We can start, and even start again, using these principles, guides and wisdom to prudently move through life at a pace which makes for success at the end of the journey. I'm approaching that end. And, I'd like to leave with my family this volume of insights into breaking the chains of fussing in relationships. Maybe, just maybe one of you will take this book, improve it, enlarge it and share it with the world so that your world will be a better place than you found it. If you notice the chart which follows, time is running out.

I know I need my wife, my children, my son-in-law and my daughter-in-law, my grandchildren, my brothers, sisters, my friends, my fellow church members, my neighbors and even strangers sometimes to show me forgiveness, grace and a kind spirit. I desire to do the same for all of them. This produces peace.

May it be so.

I hope this book helps!

ADDENDUM

10 / 5 / 10 / 5 TECHNIQUE

First Speaker   10 minutes

    Share the burden, problem, core of disagreement

Second Speaker   5 minutes

    Respond to only what has been said at this time

Second Speaker   10 minutes

    Share the burden, problem core of disagreement

First Speaker   5 minutes

    Respond to what the Second speaker said at this
    time

**(modified technique from : Prep Inc., as shared by
Dr. Rod Marshall.)**

Together come to a consensus:

1. We can understand and forgive
2. We need more time to think about it and set a time to talk again
3. We need help with our communication to and with each other / pastor; professional counsellor
4. We will work together on the problem until it is resolved to the satisfaction of both parties.

APPENDIX

Timeline for the Second Coming of Christ and Related Events

Creation
<<

Messiah Prophesied

Birth of Christ

Christ's Death on Cross

Christ's Ascension

Holy Spirit Descends

Church on Mission . . . .

3 1/2

Rapture of Church

Saints in New Heaven

Judgment Seat of Christ

Tribulation

Consummation

3 1/2

Great White Throne

Satan loosed for a little season

Satan and Hell

LAW

[--- Church AGE---------GRACE----------][--7 years Trib--][-- 1,000 years--]-------?]

1900 years +

Keys of the Kingdom

Ben Chandler

251

Fuss! Fuss! Fuss!

Will you take

The challenge of

"Dying to self"

<u>and</u>

"Knowing when to stand?"

_____ Yes, I will !

Made in the USA
Columbia, SC
16 February 2023

12157179R00146